D1453597

SATAN'S GUNS

Center Point
Large Print

Also by James Clay and available from
Center Point Large Print:

Devil's Due
Gunfighter's Revenge
Songbird of the West

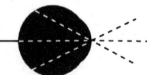

SATAN'S GUNS

A Western Adventure

James Clay

CENTER POINT LARGE PRINT
THORNDIKE, MAINE

This Center Point Large Print edition
is published in the year 2022 by arrangement with
the author.

The text of this Large Print edition is unabridged.
In other aspects, this book may vary
from the original edition.
Printed in the United States of America
on permanent paper.
Set in 16-point Times New Roman type.

ISBN: 978-1-63808-221-7

The Library of Congress has cataloged this record
under Library of Congress Control Number: 2021948535

SATAN'S GUNS

Chapter One

Reverend Colt felt tense as he rode into the town of Grayson, Texas. Tension was nothing new to the gunfighter but this was different. He was starting a new life, or going back to the old one. He wasn't quite sure which.

Lanterns lit up the town, helped by yellow glares gushing over the bat wings of Grayson's saloons. The gunfighter was familiar with the town. A man he vaguely recognized was making his way along the boardwalk, and gave Colt a quick wave. The gunfighter returned the gesture, grateful the man had not called out his name. Colt couldn't remember exactly who the gent was, maybe a store owner . . .

He reined up in front of the office of the *Grayson Herald*. His tension began to dissipate. Inside the office were two people who had, in so many ways, saved his life. The shade was pulled down on the Herald's one window but the flickering yellow border indicated Phineas and Mandy Wilsey were working inside.

A smile made its way across Reverend Colt's angular face as he dismounted and tied up his cayuse at a hitch rail. Phineas Wilsey had spent much of his life trying to find a nickname to replace "Phineas." Over the last year he had at last succeeded. People had begun calling him "Scoop" because of the claims he often made in the Herald that the paper was printing a scoop. Those claims were often exaggerated and the nickname was given with affectionate humor by the townspeople, but Phineas had happily grabbed it.

Colt's gunfighter instincts were overwhelmed by his sudden good mood. As he approached the office door he paid little heed to the sounds of nervous scampering that came from inside the office.

"Hello, Scoop!" Reverend Colt shouted as he stepped inside and faced Scoop Wilsey. Scoop was standing against the far wall of the office. His boyish face was ashen and he didn't speak.

"What's—" Colt's hand began to move toward his gun but was stopped by an explosion of red which started inside his head and then collapsed his legs. He fought for consciousness and rolled on the floor to escape the attacker who continued to come at him. The gunfighter tried to piece together what was happening as he looked up, and through blurred vision, saw his gun twirling toward the opposite side of the office and the dark barrel of a six-shooter pointing directly at him.

Something between a laugh and a squeal pierced the office. "This here Reverend Colt is becomin' a holy roller! Pick the holy roller up, boys, and put him in a chair."

Nausea shot through Colt as he was roughly lifted and slammed onto a hard wooden chair. The gunfighter's vision began to clear and what he saw brought him no comfort.

"Kid Madero," Colt said to the figure that sneered at him from a few feet away. The gunfighter reflected to himself that, in this case, the handle of "Kid" had it right. Kid Madero, while large and muscular, was sixteen. The story went that Kid Madero killed his first man when he was twelve. Colt had no trouble believing it.

Madero, as always, was adorned in expensive clothes: a black suit, string tie and a derby. His handsome face had a look of being chiseled to perfection and was topped by blond hair. Two shiny holsters wrapped around his waist. One holster held a pearl handled Smith and Wesson. Its twin was in Madero's hand.

The kid had two accomplices. Both were about his age and while strong appearing, they lacked Madero's build and swagger. Their clothes in no way matched that of their leader. Kid Madero didn't tolerate competition.

"That's right, Colt, you and I brushed by each other in Houston a while back but never got acquainted. Well, you're gonna learn a lot 'bout me before this night is over. You're gonna learn all those stories 'bout me is true. I'm a right mean fella." Madero switched his gaze to Scoop Wilsey. "Let that pretty little lady of yours loose."

The outlaw's words carried a strong threat. He was saying the "pretty little lady" was part of the scheme to prove he was a "mean fella."

Scoop opened a closet door and Mandy Wilsey stepped out, a small dog brushing her ankles as it walked beside her. Her beautiful face was tear stained and her usually well combed, dark brown hair was disheveled. "Reverend Colt, I'm sorry, I tried to warn you but—"

Madero interrupted the young woman. "But her husband had the good sense to put her and the mutt in the closet before Dencel here had hisself a good time with his knife."

Kid Madero briefly waved his gun in the direction of Dencel who stood on one side of Reverend Colt. "Dencel ain't much when it comes to firearms. Hell, he couldn't hit the broad side of a barn. But, oh my, is he ever good with a knife."

Madero smiled mockingly at his three prisoners. "You folks will have to excuse my bad manners, I plum forgot to make introductions. The jasper standin' on the other side of our guest of honour is Judd. Now, Judd handles that .44 he's holdin' somethin' fine. So, we got ourselves here the makin's of a right nice party."

Colt's eyes flared as he spoke. "Madero, if you hurt Mandy or Scoop, I'll kill you."

The outlaw replied with a cruel laugh. "My, my, Preacher, seems you're havin' trouble turnin' the other cheek. You're supposed to be endin' your gunfighter days and headin' back to a pull-pit."

"Sending you to Hell would do more good than any sermon I could preach."

"I think the Reverend is startin' to git his strength back." Madero looked at his two henchmen. "Tie him up."

Dencel took a few steps backwards toward a desk and the rope that was lying on it. Colt eyed Judd who was giving Mandy a leering look over. The gunfighter slammed his hand against Judd's wrist. As Judd dropped the gun, Colt bolted to his feet and dropped Judd with a hard blow to the side of his head.

"Look out!" Mandy shouted.

Colt turned around in time to see Dencel charging at him with a knife. He grabbed the knife arm and the two men began a grotesque dance as Colt tried to take away the weapon. Dencel was powerful. Colt could see Judd getting back up but there was little he could do about it.

Kid Madero took several quick steps toward the fight as Judd, now back on his feet, slammed his pistol against his adversary's head. While the outlaws watched Reverend Colt crumble, Scoop charged toward Madero. The attempt was hopeless. Madero took a step backward and tripped the newspaperman.

The small dog ran at Madero and bit him in the ankle. A ferocious anger filled Madero's eyes as he gave the dog a hard kick. The small animal yelped in pain as it shot up into the air then hit the floor. Madero cocked his pistol and aimed it at the animal.

"Clyde!" Mandy shouted as both she and her husband scrambled toward the dog which now whined in pain. They stood over the animal, placing themselves between Clyde and his would be killer.

Madero pointed his gun at the couple. "Both of ya git away. I'm gonna shut that mutt up with a bullet to—"

"No boss!" Judd yelled. "We're makin' too much noise the way it is, a shot will bring the law."

An icy, sullen look swept over Kid Madero's face. His henchman was right but the kid wasn't about to admit it. He did a quick glance around him. Reverend Colt was lying on the floor unconscious. The two Wilseys were still standing in front of the dog, while looking in a concerned manner toward Colt. Dencel and Judd were standing over their fallen prisoner awaiting instructions.

"We gotta git to the Ward ranch!" Madero proclaimed angrily as if someone had made a contrary suggestion.

Scoop's voice rose in surprise. "You mean

Jared and Sally Ward? Why are we going there?"

The question allowed Kid to reassert his mock-friendly persona. He spoke as he carefully uncocked his pistol. "Why, Jared and Sally is right fine Christian folks who helped to git the Reverend back on the straight and narrow. Seems only right for all of us to pay 'em a neighborly visit."

"Jared Ward isn't even home," Mandy said. "He and his hands are taking a herd of horses to Fort—"

Madero again dropped the friendly façade. "I know that! Jus' keep your mouth shut and do what I tell ya! Dencel, tie the Reverend up."

As Dencel followed instructions, Judd spoke quickly to Mandy and Scoop. "There's a buckboard out back along with your horses and ours. We're puttin' Colt on the flatbed under a tarp. We'll ride outta town together." He pointed his gun directly at Scoop. "You're gonna be talkin' friendly-like with the boss man. Anyone sees us leavin' will think we're on a social call. Remember, Dencel will be drivin'. I'll be ridin' with the lady. Do somethin' stupid and I'll kill your wife. Sure hate to rip open such a beautiful creature but I will."

Scoop nodded his head. The journalist was desperately trying to understand their captors in hopes of outsmarting them. Of course, Kid Madero was the leader but he was erratic and could easily lose control. Judd was the man who kept things moving along. It appeared that Dencel's one joy in life was using his knife. How could he and Mandy overcome such overwhelming brutality?

The reporter silently admitted to himself that the next action might have looked funny had the circumstances not been so horrible. With Dencel and Judd carrying a bound Reverend Colt out the back door, Mandy was tying a cloth around the gunfighter's head to stop the bleeding.

Madero's cold empty eyes pierced the newspaperman ending such whimsical thoughts. Madero motioned with his gun for Scoop to follow the parade. Kid Madero was the last out and slammed the door behind him.

Outside, behind the newspaper office, Scoop spotted a reason for slight hope. Pecos was sitting three buildings up behind the Mule Kick Saloon, his back against the building. To a casual observer the man looked passed out. But Scoop could see Pecos's head bobbing back and forth. He was getting ready to sing.

Pecos liked to sing when he got drunk. The patrons of the Mule Kick couldn't stand his warbling and would shout at him to leave. Pecos would self-righteously condemn everyone in the saloon for their philistine lack of artistic judgement, then take his bottle out back where he delivered a private performance for the alley cats.

Judd and Dencel were placing Colt on the buckboard as Mandy made sure the bandage around his head would hold. Scoop spoke to Kid Madero in a loud voice but not loud enough to raise suspicion. "Why are we going to the Ward ranch?"

Madero's attention was focused on his henchmen. "Jus' do what you're told."

The reporter persisted. "But why go see Jared and Sally Ward?"

"I tole ya ta shut up!"

Scoop shut up as he and his wife mounted their steeds. As ordered, Scoop and Kid Madero rode on one side of the buckboard with Judd and Mandy across from them. As they rode past the Mule Kick Saloon, the reporter could hear Pecos begin to bellow out, *Beautiful Dreamer*. But no one else seemed to notice as Pecos's warbling blended with the clatter of the buckboard.

There was still a slight hope.

Chapter Two

"Stop right here!" Kid Madero gave the order as the buckboard was about twenty yards from the Ward ranch house.

Madero drew his gun and pointed it across the wagon at Mandy. "Judd, while I keep an eye on the lady, you check on our guest of honour. If he's still napping, wake him up!"

"Right, boss," Judd snapped his reply.

Madero didn't even bother to eye Scoop Wilsey. With his gun pointed at the newspaperman's wife, he knew Scoop wouldn't cause trouble.

As he watched Judd dismount, Scoop pegged the boy's age at about sixteen, Dencel might be younger. These kids should be in school, he thought, acting goofy around girls, and taking advantage of their last chance to be free of most adult responsibilities.

But they were killers who had crossed a line from which they couldn't turn back. Wilsey remembered his own school days; the cruelty of the tricks the boys had played on each other. That cruelty had totally seized these three boys. Mandy, Reverend Colt and he were prisoners of brutal monsters.

"Wakey, wakey," Judd mocked as he began to pull Reverend Colt from the wagon.

"Hold it!" Madero ordered as he turned to Dencel who was still sitting on the buckboard's bench. "Toss Judd your knife."

Resentment filled Dencel's face. "I want it right back!"

"You'll get it back," Madero replied in a sharp whisper that was almost a hiss. "Now, toss Judd the knife!"

Dencel tossed but Judd didn't catch. He allowed the weapon to drop near his feet then picked it up. That action reaped a string of muttered obscenities from Dencel.

"Cut the Reverend's feet loose," Madero instructed his henchman. "We're all of us gonna walk up to the ranch house. Judd and Dencel, you keep back with Colt. The Wilseys will knock on the door. I'll be standin' right behind them with a big smile on my face and a gun in my hand. Ever'one unnerstand?"

The kid's gang members and his prisoners all nodded their heads. Scoop noted that Reverend Colt, now standing on his feet, appeared lucid but very weak.

Those who were on horseback dismounted and then tied their steeds to the buckboard. Dencel hopped off the wagon, ran toward Judd and retrieved his knife. He looked the weapon over with an intense parental concern. Satisfied no harm had been done, he slid the knife into a holster on his belt.

Madero straightened his string tie and adjusted his derby while keeping his Smith and Wesson pointed at the Wilseys. "Now, I expect you folks to act proper like. You're callin' on Missus Sally and bringin' a friend along. Let's get movin'."

They walked slowly toward the ranch house. As they reached the steps of the front porch, Scoop looked behind him quickly. Kid Madero appeared to be a fine gentleman, a wealthy young businessman. The hand holding the gun was hidden under his coat but, somehow, Madero made it look natural. A wide, friendly grin covered his handsome face.

Scoop knocked on the door, and listened as Sally's footsteps approached. The pudgy, gray haired lady opened the door and gazed pleasantly at her guests. She enjoyed having company.

"Mandy, Scoop, it's wonderful to see you. Please come in." She smiled and motioned with her hand, at Kid Madero indicating that the invitation included him.

Sally Ward remained in the open doorway, looking at the three men approaching her. "Why, . . . that's Reverend Colt."

"Yes, ma'am, it is," Madero spoke politely.

A look of concern came over Ward's face as the threesome drew near. "He looks like he's been hurt."

"Yes, ma'am," Madero repeated, "he's beat up right bad."

Sally Ward had been brought up in the West. She recognized the two men who almost dragged Reverend Colt into the house as hardcases. A frightened gasp escaped her mouth as she saw that Colt's hands were tied behind his back.

"Sally, I'm so sorry, we didn't want—" Mandy went silent as Kid Madero pulled his gun out from beneath his coat.

Sally looked first at the weapon, then at the man holding it. "What is the meaning of this?!"

A vicious smile cut across Madero's face. "Now, ma'am, you shouldn't go actin' all ornery. We're guests in your house. Besides, I'm gonna see to it that you got nothin' to fret about."

Madero fired a bullet directly into Sally Ward's face. Mandy screamed as her friend's body lurched backwards then dropped to the ground, blood splattering into the air and then onto the floor.

The Wilseys embraced. Madero approached his victim's corpse as it convulsed. "Look how she's floppin' about, fellas, jus' like a chicken with its head cut off!"

Laughter from the three boys screeched over the living room. Reverend Colt shouted in anger. "You just killed an unarmed woman, Madero. What kind of man are you?"

Madero stopped laughing. "I'm a man who wants to be taken serious."

"What do you mean?" Colt fired back. Judd

and Dencel stood on each side of Colt ready to inflict another assault.

"I mean, you're gonna die before this night is over, Reverend. Yep, you're gonna be enterin' those pearly gates." Madero pressed his lips together and his mouth twitched like a snake under a lifted rock. The last part of his statement had unsettled him.

He suddenly laughed again. "But, we're gonna make sure you get a strong taste of Hell before you leave this earth. This is gonna be the most awful night of your life."

Kid Madero turned to the Wilseys who were still holding each other. "Now, things might go better for you two. But you best do what I say, if you don't wanna end up like Missus Sally Ward."

"When are we gettin' to the good stuff, boss?" Dencel's voice had the whiny quality of an impatient child.

"Right now!" Madero almost shouted his reply. "Dencel, Judd, find the Reverend somethin' to sit on, and stay beside him, makin' sure he can see the show." He stared for a moment at the Wilseys as if envying the genuine intimacy between them. "Mister Wilsey, I want you to get over there with the Reverend, Judd and Dencel."

"What have you—"

Madero cut off Scoop's response. "You heard me!" He nodded toward the dead body on the floor. "You do what I say, no questions!"

21

Scoop made his way to where Colt was now sitting on a footstool. As had been the case in the office, Dencel and Judd bookended him. Scoop reluctantly stood by Judd.

Kid Madero's tongue ran over the top of his mouth as he stared straight ahead at Mandy. "Take off your clothes, lady."

Dencel laughed gleefully. He almost jumped up and down in anticipation.

Mandy's voice trembled but was still defiant. "I won't."

Madero's voice oozed confidence. "Yes, you will, unless you wanna see your husband join Missus Sally there on the floor. I bet his body will go floppin' about too!"

Mandy tried an appeal to her captor's compassion. "Why are you doing these terrible things to us?"

Madero took a step closer to Mandy. "All sorts of reasons, some of them is business. But, there's more to it. You see, I ain't goin' to the pearly gates, not after all what I done. So, after you take your clothes off, we're gonna tie you to the bed. I'm gonna have my Heaven right here tonight."

Chapter Three

Rance Dehner twirled the reins of his horse around a hitch rail, stepped onto a boardwalk and made his way into the sheriff's office. A huge man, well over six feet and heavy set, stood behind a desk scattered with wanted posters, government forms, a partially eaten sandwich, an open bottle of sarsaparilla, a small bag of gumdrops and a newspaper.

"Howdy!" The big man's greeting was friendly.

Dehner repeated the greeting, and continued to speak as he shook hands with the man who towered over the desk. "The name's Rance Dehner, I'm a detective with the Lowrie Agency, are you the sheriff?"

"I am for the time bein'." The sheriff pushed some government forms aside, picked up a sheriff's badge and pinned it on his vest. "I shined this thing a few hours ago, then forgot 'bout it. Grayson used to have us a fine sheriff but he kicked off two months back. Natural causes. I miss him, of course, but I think it kinda nice when a lawdog dies natural like, do ya know what I mean?"

"I think so, Sheriff . . ."

"Ox Bently, jus' call me Ox, ever'one does." He picked up the bag of gumdrops, took one and tilted the bag to Dehner, who mouthed a thank you as he pulled out a sugary treat.

"I've lived in Grayson most my life," the sheriff said as he rolled the candy around in his mouth. "Done most ever' thing. Been a bartender, preacher, deputy sheriff, even cleaned out stables for a while, right now I'm the mayor and I own two saloons and the livery."

"Sounds like you've climbed the ladder of success."

Ox paused as if pondering the truth of Rance's statement. "Reverend Colt, he's an educated fella, Boston and all, he's called me a Renaissance Man, I think that's a compliment."

"Yes, it is." Rance changed the subject. "I get the impression your official title is acting sheriff."

"Your impression is plum right. Monday, Zeke Talbot will come in on the stage, it'll be his last time ridin' shotgun. He'll be my deputy for a few weeks, then I'll give him this badge I jus' polished."

"Zeke's bones getting a bit weary of riding a stagecoach?" Dehner asked.

"Well, Zeke rides beside Cactus Olsen. Cactus is a good driver and a friendly old cuss but he fought for the Confederacy and loves to jaw 'bout how he single handed like won jus' 'bout ever' battle that got fought. A few weeks ago, Zeke asked him 'If you were such a great hero how come the Confederacy lost the war?' They ain't got along very well since."

Dehner nodded his head and again changed the subject. "I'm afraid I've got some bad news, Sheriff."

"That's the kind I most git."

"I'm trailing Kid Madero and two thugs that are riding with him," Dehner explained. "There's a good chance they may be in Grayson. Madero is wanted—"

"I know all 'bout that snake, if—"

"Sheriff!" A short middle-aged man came running into the office.

"Yeh, what is it, Tom?"

Tom Bascomb paused trying to get his thoughts in order, before speaking. "Just a while back, I saw Reverend Colt riding into town. He stopped at the Herald office."

Ox shrugged his shoulders. "Yeh, Scoop and Mandy knew he was comin'."

Tom began to gesture frantically with his hands. "Well, seeing him head for the newspaper office, I recalled I hadn't got my advertisement for the next edition to the Wilseys yet. So, I went to the store and wrote it up . . . I'm having a sale on fencing—"

Ox cut in. "I'll read 'bout it in the paper, keep on tellin' me what happened!"

Bascomb clapped his hands together in a prayerful manner. "When I got there everyone was gone and Clyde was lying on the floor bleeding!"

"Who's Clyde?" Dehner asked.

Ox's face went pale. "He's a dog that belongs to Scoop and Mandy, they love him and would never . . . I gotta get over there!"

Ox ran from the office with Tom and Rance immediately behind him. The detective noted that for such a large man, Ox could run fast and it didn't require a detective to deduct that Ox thought highly of the two newspaper people. This matter was personal to the sheriff.

The lawman stormed into the newspaper office, ran directly to the dog and shouted an order at Bascomb, "Take Clyde over to Doc Cranston's place!"

"But Doc Cranston is a people doctor he—"

"Cranston loves Clyde as much as the Wilseys do, get movin'!"

As Tom obeyed the lawman's command, Ox did a quick survey of the newspaper office. "The dog weren't the only one bleedin'." He followed drops of blood to the back door and quickly went through it.

"There's blood on the ground here and look at those tracks," he said to Dehner who was right behind him.

"A buckboard and several horses . . . do you know anyone who would want to abduct the newspaper people?" the detective asked.

A pale look of alarm covered Ox's face. "Naaa, and what's worse, I don't know where they woulda took 'em."

A bellow suddenly sounded from nearby. "Oh Suzanna, dun't ya cry fer me, I come from Alabamy . . ."

Ox ran toward Pecos who was still sitting behind the Mule Kick. Dehner once again trailed behind the lawman.

Pecos did not appreciate the attention. "Ah, Ox, dun't a-rest me ag'in I ain't—"

The sheriff cut him off. "How long ya been here, Pecos?"

"I ain't a man who puts much store in keepin' time, Ox."

"Have ya seen anythin' unusual-like behind the newspaper office?"

A look of recognition wavered across the glassy vagueness of Pecos's eyes. "Yeh, the newspaper fella and his pretty wife, they was with a lotta folks, some of 'em got on a wagon the others on horses."

Ox snapped a quick response. "Where did they go?"

Pecos waved an arm in all directions, "That way!"

"Damn it, Pecos, this is important. Think man, did you hear anyone say where they was goin'."

The urgency in Ox's voice touched something deep and ugly in Pecos. Even with a brain half-

27

ruined by alcohol he had clung to a warped sense of self-preservation. Booze wasn't free and every chance to demand a quick, dirty dollar needed to be grabbed.

"Ya know, Ox, it jus' might be I heard somethin' but my thinkin' is sorta tired, maybe with a little in-spi-ration . . ."

Ox handed him a coin. Pecos placed it in his shirt pocket as a wicked, hungry smile cut his face. "I kin feel my ol' brain startin' to chug up a bit, but it seems to need more fuel, maybe . . ."

The sheriff grabbed the filthy collar of Pecos's shirt, thrust a knuckle into his windpipe and pressed the drunkard against the back wall of the saloon. "Ya tell me what ya know now, Pecos, or I'll break your worthless neck!"

Pecos choked his words out. "OK, OK, I was only joshin'."

The lawman let go. "Stop joshin' and get serious. Fast!"

Pecos took a few deep breaths before answering, "Ward ranch, that's where they was headin'."

The sheriff's face crunched. "The Ward ranch . . . why there?"

The drunk held up a shaking arm in front of his face. "Dun't know, honest!"

"I believe him," Dehner said.

Ox nodded agreement, "I'm goin' after 'em. You wanna come along?"

"Yes."

"They're usin' a buckboard that'll slow 'em down." Once again, Ox began to run. "Let's git to the livery, we're gonna need fresh horses."

Chapter Four

Both Ox and Dehner were on roans and both horses were lathered as they pulled up beside the buckboard standing twenty yards or so from the Ward ranch house.

"Ya put a lotta store in coincidence, Rance?"

"Not too much."

"I'm the same." Like Dehner, Ox spoke in a low voice as both men quietly dismounted. "Ya trailed Kid Madreo and his buzzards to Grayson. There's a beat up dog in the newspaper office and blood all over the place. Scoop and Mandy is missin'." Ox lifted the tarp on the bed of the buckboard. "There's more blood here. Ask me, it all comes together."

"What about this Reverend Colt?"

"I ain't got that quite figgered yet but I think he's got hisself mixed up in it." Bently looked toward the ranch house. "I kin see shadows on the curtains. Sally's got herself quite a few callers."

"What do you want to do?"

"The house has a large winda on each side. Ya go right, I'll take the left. After that, we'll sorta do what we gotta." Both men drew their guns as they quickly and stealthily carried out the lawman's plan.

As Ox reached his destination, he had no

trouble assessing the situation. Laced curtains had been tied back earlier in the day allowing residents a good view of the heavens. But the view inside was hellish. Sally Ward lay in a pool of blood. Only because he recognized her dress could Ox be sure it was Sally.

Reverend Colt was sitting on a stool of some kind with a bandage around his head. A gunman, who had a knife holstered in his belt held a pistol near Colt. Another gunman bookended Reverend Colt, his revolver drawn, but this owlhoot seemed more interested in Scoop Wilsey who twitched nervously on the other side of the thug as if looking for an opening to attack.

In the midst of the horror stood Mandy Wilsey, facing a well dressed man, Ox immediately realized was Kid Madero. Madero had a gun pointed at the young woman. Bently could only take quick glances inside to avoid detection but he did spot Rance Dehner at the opposite window. Dehner had impressed the sheriff as a good man to have on your side when matters got rough. He hoped he was right.

The lawman was crouched under the window when he heard Madero's voice. "Let me explain this polite-like one more time, pretty lady. You're gonna pleasure us tonight, one way or another. Now, if you git ornery 'bout it, I'll kill your husband. If you cooperate and start takin' off your clothes right now, jus' maybe I'll be a bit nicer."

Ox rose to where his eyes could see through the bottom of the window. Mandy was trembling as she spoke, "All right, all right." Her fingers moved to the buttons on her blouse.

"No!" Scoop ran toward Madero. Judd cocked the hammer of his gun and pointed at Wilsey. Reverend Colt bolted up and slammed his body against the killer causing his shot to burrow into the ceiling. Judd angrily fired a bullet into Colt, who, hands tied, spun and then dropped to the floor.

"Had enough of you!" Judd again cocked his revolver and, this time pointed it downward at Colt. Dehner fired through the window. A muffled sound of glass shattering pierced through Judd's hearing which had been deadened by the gunshots. It would be the final sound he heard on earth. He was dead before he hit the ground.

"Not fair! Not fair!" Dencel shouted as he fired a wild shot at Dehner.

The detective didn't know exactly what his adversary meant and gave it little thought. Dencel stood close by the man with his hands tied whose body twisted in pain as he lay helpless on the floor. Dehner lanced two bullets into Dencel's chest. Dencel dropped his gun, staggered about and seemed to be trying to reach for his knife as he collapsed.

Kid Madero fired at Dehner as Scoop tackled him causing the shot to go into a wall. The two men hit the floor. The reporter grabbed the gun from Madero's hand but the outlaw twisted Scoop's arm, causing him to drop the weapon. Madero then pushed his adversary away as he picked up the Smith and Wesson and scrambled to his feet.

Scoop started to get up but Mandy had spotted the two men at the windows and immediately recognized Ox. "Stay down!" The young woman jumped on her husband as guns fired from both windows.

Madero's body gyrated crazily, as his face appeared to bulge more from shock than pain. He gave a loud, beseeching screech and for the first time that night Dehner remembered Kid Madero was only sixteen. The outlaw suddenly went silent and then fell to the floor.

Dehner and Bently climbed through the windows as Mandy and Scoop holding on to each other, returned to their feet and then hastily moved toward Reverend Colt. Ox hustled toward the threesome and began to cautiously free Colt's hands.

Dehner inspected the bodies on the floor, as the sharp acrid smell of gunpowder filled his lungs. *That odor is becoming too familiar,* the detective grimly reflected.

From a previous encounter, Rance recognized Judd and Dencel, both of whom were dead as was the lady, whose head was almost gone. The smoke filling the room began to settle downwards as the detective crouched over Kid Madero and discovered he was breathing.

Blood gave Madero's lips a clownish appearance as he lifted his head slightly. "Dehner . . . thought we'd lost you . . ."

"You're not as good at covering a trail as you thought, Kid," Rance bluntly stated. "You were never good at a lot of things."

Bitterness caused the killer's lips to curl. His teeth were covered by a coat of red. "You're no hero, Dehner, you ain't saved Reverend Colt."

Blood dribbled out the side of Madero's mouth. There was little time left and Rance needed to get all the information he could. "What do you mean?"

The Kid's speech was now becoming a gurgle. "Colt gonna die slow and awful."

"Who says?"

Smoke began to form a cocoon around Kid Madero and seemed to be pulling him down as he returned his head to the floor. "Satan . . . Satan."

The cocoon now took the appearance of a coffin. Rance felt a hand on his shoulder. "Is he gone?" Bently asked.

"Yes," Dehner replied as he rose. "So are his friends."

"Rance, I'm sorry I had ta let ya do most of the shootin'."

"Madero was in your line of fire when Judd

was getting ready to shoot the tied up prisoner, so was the lady."

"Yeh, but shootin' someone from ambush, no warnin' or nothin', it leaves a bad feelin' in your gut."

Dehner nodded his head and said nothing.

"The prisoner, Reverend Colt, we need to get him back to town and to the doc's real quick."

"Sure." Rance patted the lawman on the back and then began to help with the wounded man. Ox quickly introduced Dehner to Mandy and Scoop, then the detective volunteered to drive the buckboard up to the front door of the house.

"Thanks for all you have done, Mr. Dehner," Mandy said. "This has been such a terrible, terrible night. Thank God, it's over."

Rance said something encouraging he didn't believe, then left the house and began to run toward the buckboard. Reverend Colt might survive his wounds but otherwise the detective thought Mandy was wrong. The terror of this night was only the beginning.

Chapter Five

Scoop Wilsey handed his wife a cup of coffee. "This will help steady your nerves a bit."

"Thank you," Mandy quietly replied.

The newspaperman affectionately squeezed his wife's shoulder before pouring coffee for Bently and Dehner. He then placed the pot on a tray which perched on a small table at the center of the gathering and sat down on a sofa with Mandy. Making and serving coffee was not a customary chore for Scoop but he knew Mandy would have felt obliged to handle the job otherwise and his wife needed rest.

The four people were sitting in the living room of the Wilsey house. Rance mused to himself that, despite the circumstances, the place did convey charm. A white picket fence fronted a small but well constructed house consisting of a living room, bedroom and kitchen.

Ox and Rance were both seated in armchairs each of which faced the sofa. There was silence as Mandy sipped coffee and closed her eyes. As her eyes opened she forced a smile for her guests. "Sorry, I'm—"

"Ya don't need to apologize for nothin'," Ox cut in. "Ya have been through . . . ah . . . a . . . very hard time."

Ox's awkward avoidance of profanity turned Mandy's smile genuine. "I have helped Doctor Cranston with surgery before but not when the patient was someone I knew as well as Reverend Colt and not after, well . . . a very hard time."

"Doc says he couldn't have done it without you," Scoop interrupted, "that bullet was hard to get out."

Mandy gently petted Clyde. The small dog, bandaged but well, lay at her feet. "The doctor isn't sure but the damage to Reverend Colt's arm may have been permanent."

Silence followed. Dehner broke it, "Could you tell me something about Reverend Colt? Is he a gunfighter or a preacher?"

"Both," Mandy answered. "His real name is Paul Colten. He was educated in Boston where he became a pastor. Paul also got married in Boston. He and his wife Christina moved to a small town in the West, Sterling, Arizona, to start a church. Paul even wrote a book called *Frontier Truths*. We have a copy of it and plan to run portions of it in the newspaper. He got the name Reverend Colt from a child who innocently mispronounced his name. That seemed funny . . . at first."

"At first?" Dehner gently prodded.

Mandy continued. "There was a very wild young man in the town, Jerry Blaine, he fancied himself a gunfighter. Paul and Christina wanted to help him. They brought him into their home and Jerry helped Paul work on repairs needed in the church."

The young woman began to fuss with her coffee. Her husband continued the narrative. "One morning, Paul was called away on an emergency. When he returned home he found that Jerry Blaine had murdered Christina after . . . violating her. Blaine had taken off and the law couldn't find him."

Mandy again picked up the story as she placed her coffee on the table. "Paul went on a personal vendetta to kill the man who had murdered his wife. It took him a while, which may have been good, because he practiced his draw every spare moment he had. When he finally caught up with Jerry Blaine, he outdrew him. After that, Paul tried to return to being a pastor but he couldn't. That is when Reverend Colt, the gun for hire was born."

"How did the gun for hire end up here in Grayson, Texas?" Dehner asked.

Mandy's eyes became misty. "He rescued my late father and myself. We ran a medicine show of sorts. We were riding into Grayson to take advantage of a town celebration when two thugs stopped us. Luckily, Paul came along. He had to kill one of the outlaws and rode into Grayson with us to make sure the other thug was jailed."

"But the sheriff back then was a dishonest skunk," Ox declared, "ta make matters worse

39

he was the puppet of an even bigger skunk. Reverend Colt helped us to run out the skunks and make this town decent."

"By 'us' Ox means himself, Mandy, and me, among others," Scoop explained. "We were able to get the good citizens of Grayson behind us but it was tough and we never could have done it without Reverend Colt. Grayson owes him a lot."

Ox smiled gently at the couple on the sofa. "But you two helped pay him back some."

A quizzical expression crunched Dehner's face. Mandy answered the silent question. "Scoop and I fell in love during all the troubles." She paused, winked at her husband and then continued. "Paul Colten came back to Grayson for our wedding. After that, he would return to town frequently."

"He helped us build that fine lookin' church at the edge of town," Ox Bently added. "Colt really impressed all the town folks, I mean a preacher doin' real work."

"There was a lot more real work going on," Mandy said. "Paul would have long discussions with Scoop and myself. He came to a better and stronger understanding of his faith and felt ready to become pastor of our town's church."

"Good thing," Ox bellowed. "I was the one doin' the preachin' at services held in the Mule Kick Saloon. I weren't much of an attraction."

Scoop worked his hands for a moment before looking at Dehner. "Please understand this,

Rance. Reverend Colt was a gun for hire, but he only went after people who needed to be jailed. Yes, he killed some of them, but they were people who had to be killed."

What Reverend Colt did isn't much different from what I do as a detective, Dehner thought but out loud settled for, "I understand. How long did Paul Colten work as a gun for hire?"

"Oh, about two and a half years, I'd say." Scoop looked at this wife who nodded agreement.

"As soon as he is up to it, we're going to have to ask Paul Colten about those two and a half years," Dehner said.

Scoop shrugged his shoulders. "Why?"

"Kid Madero and his bunch weren't like Reverend Colt, they would kill anyone for money," Dehner explained. "And someone paid them to not only kill Colt but, from what you have told me, to make the last hours of his life a long, slow torture. Madero and his gang are dead but the person who hired them is alive."

Ox's voice was almost a shout. "We gotta find out who that buzzard is, it's probably someone who was close to one of them no-goods the Reverend sent to their reward."

Scoop gently petted Clyde for a few moments then looked up at the detective. "Rance, you were the last one to talk to Kid Madero. He must have known he was dying. Did he tell you anything that might be helpful?"

Dehner spoke softly, "Madero mumbled the name of 'Satan' twice."

Mandy shook her head as if dismissing the matter. "He was thinking about what was waiting for him. That probably won't help us much."

"Probably not," Dehner replied but he really didn't believe it.

Chapter Six

The next morning, a Wednesday, found Rance Dehner riding back to the Ward ranch with Ox Bently. As they left the Wilsey house the previous night Ox had said, "I gotta git back to the Wards' place early tomorra mornin'. Jared's due back soon and I don't want him to walk in and see Sally and all—"

"I'll ride with you," Dehner said.

" 'Preciate it."

Bently planned to employ the same buckboard Kid Madero had used the night before but Dehner requested a bigger wagon. "We need to bring all four bodies back to town."

"I thought we'd jus' plant those owlhoots somewhere 'round the ranch," the lawman explained. "No headstones or nothin' needed for that trash."

Rance explained why they needed to do things differently.

Rance and Ox Bently were drawing near the Ward ranch when the detective lifted his hand in a signal to stop. As the sheriff looked at him questionably Dehner removed the field glasses from his saddlebags, gazed through them for a couple of minutes and then handed the glasses to Ox who was driving the buckboard.

"Take a look at the front window."

"Ya got good eyes," Ox spoke softly while gazing through the glasses. "There's at least two fellas in the house. They moved back the front curtains probably ta git some light. They seem ta be lookin' for somethin'."

"Let's not interrupt their hard work just yet," Dehner replied. "Let's leave the buckboard and horses here. We can check on the visitors through the side windows, I'll take the right you take the left."

Ox grinned at his companion. "Sure makes me feel good to know a detective with the Lowrie Agency is usin' perty much the same plan as I had last night."

"Exactly the same plan, only remember now the glass in those windows is broken."

Both men moved to their positions. Gazing through the window, Rance saw a man with a long beard wearing old overalls, a floppy hat and no shirt going through bureau drawers. He seemed indifferent to the gruesome spectacle and odour of the dead bodies which surrounded him.

Another man with a shorter beard and a checkered shirt hanging over patched corduroy pants came running from what Dehner figured was a bedroom. A large hole near the top of his hat was the only thing that distinguished it from that of his companion. "Ross, look what all I found me."

44

The newcomer dropped a load of stuff on the bureau and the men began to look through the pile. "You done good, Willie. I ain't found nothin' here 'ceptin' papers."

Willie held up what appeared to be an ornate jewel box and shook it. "Bet there's lotta valuables in here."

"Mightin' be but fancy stuff kin be hard to sell," Ross lamented. "Only rich folks is interested and they don't take much to weuns. Now, them pipes may git us some money. There's some real high hat tobaccee here too."

Ross looked toward the front window. "Let's git us over to the barn, leave the pipes and stuff here, we'll come back fer it. At the barn, we maybe kin find us some horses and saddles . . . them always sell good ta men who ain't fussy 'bout where what they're buyin' came from."

Rance exchanged quick glances across the room with Ox Bently. The sheriff gestured to follow the intruders out to the barn.

As Ross and Willie began to leave the house, Dehner took note of their weaponry. Ross had an ancient cracked holster tied with a rope around his midsection. The gun it held, from what Dehner could tell, appeared as old as the holster.

Willie picked up a Winchester he had propped beside the bureau. From the distinctive yellow colouring surrounding the trigger, Rance pegged it as a Yellow Boy, the first rifle Winchester produced after Oliver Fisher Winchester started the company in 1866, almost fifteen years before.

"These gents are a walking museum," the detective whispered to himself.

Trailing behind the thieves was not a tough task. Neither Ross nor Willie looked back as they made their way to the barn. After opening the barn doors they left them open. Which Dehner reckoned made sense, the thieves didn't plan on a long stay.

"Ain't much here," Ross sounded disappointed as the two men entered the large structure.

"Well remember last night in town the jaspers in the saloon, the ones jawin' about Kid Madero and all, they says the boss man had left with all the hands to take the horses somewhere. That's how weuns knewed to come and have a look see."

"Recon so," Ross agreed. "But there is a few horses in the stalls and . . . wowee . . . look at the saddle lyin' on that first stall."

Dehner and the sheriff entered the barn. Without drawing his gun, Ox Bently shouted, "Both of you fools, drop your guns on the floor, stand still and put your hands up."

"Run!" Ross shouted though both thieves looked confused as to exactly where to run to. Willie darted toward the back of the barn, Ross headed for a ladder that led up to a hayloft.

Bently's shouts became louder. "Idiots, give

46

up now and nothin' serious will happen to ya."

Both Ross and Willie continued their efforts to evade the law. Bently shook his head. "Rance, could ya go after that buzzard in the hayloft? I'll take care of his buddy down here."

"Sure, but be careful, both of these jaspers have guns."

Ox smirked agreement and took off after Willie. Rance made his way hastily up the ladder. Ross was stumbling through the hay to reach the double doors at the center of the loft. Reaching the doors he slid off the wooden bar that kept them together. Pushing the doors open he looked out hoping to see a large hay wagon below.

There was nothing below except hard ground.

Dehner stopped a few feet from his adversary. "Come with me, Ross. The sheriff wants to have a chit-chat with you."

Self-righteousness blanketed Ross's face. "I ain't done nothin' wrong. Jus' takin' some things them rich people dun't need no how."

"Yep, you're a real Robin Hood, come on!"

"Make me!" Ross began to reach for his gun. Dehner lurched forward and grabbed his adversary's arm, reached into his holster, and tossed the gun out the open doors.

Ross broke loose from the grip and attempted to catch the gun in midair. He stumbled and plunged out of the barn, hitting the ground about the same time the gun arrived there.

Dehner made a fast scramble to the ladder. Going down he saw Ox pulling Willie along with one hand and holding the Yellow Boy in another. "Ross stepped out for a moment," the detective declared as he bolted outdoors and ran around to the side of the barn.

Dehner drew his gun before turning the corner to the back of the building. Who could guess what notions were plowing through Ross's head? Dehner wasn't going to try.

But the caution wasn't necessary. Ross was limping about muttering curses. The look of self-righteousness returned as he faced the detective. "My leg's broke I need me a doc and you're gonna pay the bill. This bein' your fault."

"You're leg's not broke and I'm sure the next doc you see will be far from here. You may have to clean the doc's house or stable to pay him. That will be the best thing that's happened to you in a long time."

Dehner picked up Ross's gun and guided him back to the front of the barn. The thief's limp was genuine but, Dehner suspected, exaggerated.

Ox was waiting in front of the barn doors with Willie. The expression on the sheriff's face was grim, his voice a bark, "Where are your horses?"

"In back of the house. Weuns left them there so as no one ridin' by would think anybody was stealin' from the house," Willie explained with pride. He seemed to be boasting about how intelligently he and his partner had planned.

Ox Bently wasn't impressed. "You two saddle bums are gettin' on those horses, ridin' off and never comin' back here again. I should arrest both of ya but I got more important stuff ta do then bother with the likes of you."

Ox and Rance escorted the thieves to their horses and watched them gradually become specks on the horizon.

"Maybe I'm gettin' old, Rance. I usta be able to laugh at trash like that, but I can't seem ta do it so much anymore."

Ox turned around and stared at the Ward ranch as if it were a shrine. "It ain't right. Jared and Sally Ward . . . the nicest people you'd ever know. Ever' Easter they'd allow us to have a sunrise service out here, pret-near the whole town showed up. There would be food and a lot of fun stuff for the kids. People would stay all day . . . wonderful memories, now . . ."

Ox fell silent. Dehner left him to his thoughts for several moments, then spoke softly. "We need to get started."

"Yep," Ox agreed. "We gotta job ta do." The strong emotions coursing through the lawman were grabbed and buried somewhere deep inside him. A process he had long ago learned in order to survive.

They wrapped the corpses in blankets and

placed them on the bed of the largest buckboard available at Bently's Livery. Ox left a note asking Jared to ride into town and see him. "It ain't the right way ta do this but I got no choice. The best thing would be ta have the preacher here ta meet Pete. But the preacher is lyin' in Doc's office sleeping off the laudanum."

Arriving back in Grayson, they left the bodies with the undertaker and then walked to the doctor's house which also served as his office. Both men were silent for most of the stroll but as they approached the doctor's front door, Ox commented, "Grayson's got a full time undertaker now, the job usta be done by the town's barber, that's progress, I guess."

"I guess," Dehner replied.

The men stepped into an empty living room which also served as a waiting room. Two muffled but loud voices came from behind a closed door. "Doc, you outta be ashamed, a man your age not makin' better coffee than this! Whatta you tryin' to do, kill your patients?"

The first voice was sharp and female. The reply was male and blustery. "I'm a doctor and this isn't a restaurant. Besides, the coffee here is free which is more than I can say about that establishment of yours!"

Ox grimaced and motioned for Dehner to follow him as he made his way toward a door to the right. The coffee debate was continuing as the lawman led Dehner into the doctor's surgery. There were three beds inside, two were empty, the other was occupied by Reverend Colt, who contrary to Ox's earlier statement, was sitting up with his arm in a sling, looking tired and weak. Beside him was a small table containing a tray of partially eaten food and a cup of coffee. Against the far wall opposite was a long cloth screen which had surrounded a bed the previous night when the doctor and Mandy operated on Colt.

Dehner observed that Doctor Cranston looked in not much better health than his patient. He stood at a little over five feet with slumped shoulders, a pale complexion and eyes that appeared constantly blood shot from years of getting little sleep. Tufts of white hair clung to his head. His age could range anywhere from fifty to eighty.

The coffee critic towered over the doctor. She stood close to six feet, with reddish brown hair brushing her shoulders. The woman's eyes were green and mischievous as if nothing she said could be taken seriously. Her neck's partially crinkled skin provided the only signal the lady was older than she appeared at first glance. She was large boned and most of her dark blue dress was covered by a white apron with a variety of food stains.

The java argument ended the moment the newcomers arrived, as if it had been a casual diversion. Ox made introductions. Dehner learned the lady was named Lolly Farnum and she owned Lolly's Fine Eats. "That's better than jus' callin' it Lolly's Restaurant, don't you think?" the lady asked.

"I'm the one who suggested the name," Ox declared proudly.

"Stop your braggin'," Lolly snapped.

The exchange was brief but Dehner thought he spied a genuine affection pass between the sheriff and the restaurant owner. A voice from the occupied bed moved his thoughts in a different direction.

"Mr. Dehner, I understand that you helped Ox to rescue the Wilseys and myself last night, thank you."

Dehner approached the bed, "You're more than welcome, and please call me Rance, Reverend—"

"Call me Paul, Paul Colten. I'm trying to get rid of the Reverend Colt handle." He nodded at the tray on the table beside him. "Lolly has graciously provided me with a wonderful breakfast but I'm starved for information." He looked directly at the lawman. "Ox, tell me everything that happened last night, and I mean everything."

Bently complied. Paul Colten nodded his appreciation, then spoke. "Lolly, could you step outside a few minutes? I need a little privacy to get dressed."

"You're staying right in that bed, Rev-Paul

Colten!" Doc Cranston pointed an accusing finger at his patient.

"You attend to physical health, Doctor, and I take care of spiritual problems," Colten explained. "Jared Ward is a good man who is going to need spiritual help. Being that help will do me a lot more good than lying in this bed feeling sorry for myself."

Lolly spoke to the doctor in a soft voice. "I'll get one of those buggies Ox has at the livery and ride with Paul out to the Ward place. The trail is pretty smooth. Someone should be there when Jared gets back. Think how awful that ride into town would be for Jared, not knowin' . . ."

Doctor Cranston sighed deeply and nodded his head.

But Paul Colten objected. "I can't let you do that, Lolly. You have a restaurant to look after."

"And I've got two helpers! It won't hurt 'em to do some real work for a change. Besides, Paul Colten, I owe you a debt I can never repay."

Lolly's last statement startled the pastor. She quickly continued. "My son, Caleb, he was a real tornado. Couldn't seem to stay outta trouble. Then, when he was seventeen he read your book, *Frontier Truths*, turned him around in a way, all my jawin' never could. Less than a year later, he joined the Texas Rangers. That was the happiest day of his life."

Dehner cupped a hand over his chin. "Caleb Farnum, the name sounds familiar."

Ox responded in a low voice he rarely employed. "Ya probably read 'bout him in the newspapers. Caleb went undercover and joined a gang of rustlers. Luck ran against him. One of them rustlers had been in a gang the Rangers rounded up six months before. The buzzard had escaped prison. He recognized Caleb and . . ."

Lolly cut in, "The Texas Rangers buried him with honours. He died a man who was doing a lot of good in this world." The woman's face began to contort. She looked away from Colten as she spoke to him. "Hurry up and make yourself decent. We gotta get out there before Jared gets back."

She pretended to brush strands of hair from her forehead as she hastily left the room.

After they had waved good-bye to the buggy as it pulled out of the livery, Dehner turned to the sheriff. "I plan to stay around town for a while, could you use a volunteer deputy?"

"Sure could! Does that agency ya work for have more work for ya here?"

"Maybe."

Dehner accompanied Ox as he did a round of Grayson pointing out various trouble spots. "No need to give it much thought. Wherever you find lots of booze and females ya can

54

always bet the atmosphere ain't too peaceful."

After the round, Ox returned to his office while Dehner headed for the clapboard structure that housed the *Grayson Herald*. Inside, he found the two Wilseys working at separate desks. Between the desks was a collection of old blankets which served as a makeshift bed for Clyde. The small dog raised his head and stared at the detective. Clyde's tail began to wag as Rance crouched over the animal and began to pet him, being careful not to touch the dog's bandages.

"Clyde seems almost as happy to see you as we were last night, Rance," Mandy said.

Dehner raised himself as he spoke. "You may not be so happy to see me today. I'm here to ask a favor."

"Name it," Scoop responded.

"I need pictures of the snakes who tried to abduct you two last night," Rance explained. "The Lowrie Agency was hired by the family of a man who was killed by Kid Madero. We need to show them a picture of Madero's corpse to prove we got him. As you know, Madero and his buddies are at the undertakers."

"Glad to help, let me get my camera," Scoop left his desk and headed for the closet which had contained his wife and dog the previous evening. "But why do you need pictures of the other two jaspers, Rance?"

"Large outfits like Wells Fargo and the railroads have what we call standing contracts out on numerous buzzards who have been causing them trouble. There's a good chance those other two may be worth a few dollars to the Lowrie Detective Agency."

Scoop carefully removed his Pearsal from the closet. "I guess it's about time they did some good for someone."

The next morning Dehner stopped by Bascomb's Emporium, which also served as a post office, and mailed the plates of the grisly pictures Scoop had taken. Tom Bascomb was obviously impressed with the address on the large envelope.

"I ain't never sent nothing to a detective agency before!" Tom declared.

"Maybe not," Dehner smiled back a reply. "But I bet you've sent and received mail from a lot of interesting places."

"Well, yes, as a matter of fact . . ."

Rance departed from the store twenty minutes later armed with a load of stories from the owner of Grayson's biggest store and its postmaster. Dehner laughed inwardly. Other detectives might spurn local gossip. But he eagerly sponged up the local talk. Yes, from a narrow stand point, much of it proved to be worthless. Still, he felt it important to understand the people he was among and sometimes an obscure, seemingly trivial remark would prove essential in solving a case.

The detective stood on the boardwalk outside the store and looked over the town. Grayson was in an early morning transition. The saloons were standing quiet while the other businesses were taking on life.

A gunshot cut through the bustling sounds. At night, one gun firing wouldn't mean much but this early in the morning . . .

A second shot made the detective realize the trouble was at Sammy's Hotel and Restaurant where he had slept the previous night and ate breakfast less than an hour before. He ran across the street, down the boardwalk, and cautiously entered the hotel's front door.

A "Back Soon" sign perched on the registration desk in the empty lobby. Loud shouts sounded from behind the double doors to Dehner's right which led to the dining area.

Dehner quickly but quietly made his way to the double doors which were located beside a stairway to the second floor. He paused as he heard a voice elevated by alcohol. "I dun't cotton to bein' lied to, where's the perty girl?"

The response came in a calm monotone spoken with an Asian accent. "Pretty girl not here right now, kindly put away gun." Dehner recognized the voice from when he had signed the hotel's register the night before: it was Sammy Wong, the establishment's owner.

"I ain't doin' nothin' kindly for any chink!"

Another shot sounded followed by a "Where's my perty girl!"

From what the detective could surmise, the bullet had been fired into the ceiling. That might not be the case with the next shot. Dehner knew that most killings in the West came from fools and drunks, not professional killers. He hurriedly took off his badge and placed it in his shirt pocket. With a plan still forming in his mind he entered the restaurant area, his Colt still holstered.

The man holding the gun was tall and muscular. At one time he had only needed to glare in order to scare off anyone who would challenge him. But booze had changed that. A large roll around his middle and an unsteady stance indicated a life gone soft and wrong. Still, the gun in his hand made him dangerous.

The other customers in the restaurant were sitting totally immobile at their tables. For a moment they reminded Rance of prairie dogs remaining perfectly still so a predator wouldn't spot them. Sammy was short and stocky with thick, dark hair. He was wearing a checkered shirt and Levi's.

Another Asian man stood in an open doorway that led to the restaurant's kitchen. He was wearing a large apron which indicated he was the cook. His gray hair was in a pigtail. He was an older man with an uncertain look on his face. Most of his right arm was out of sight, blocked by the kitchen wall. Dehner figured the cook was holding a knife or ax and wondering if he could use it successfully. Dehner hoped the question would go unanswered.

Dehner laughed as if amused by what he saw. "Good morning, friend, looks like my staff isn't treating you so well."

The gunny looked confused. "Yore staff?"

"Sure," Dehner gave a caustic laugh. "You don't think these jaspers own anything, do you?"

The gunny looked at the two Asian men with contempt. "Guess not."

"My name is Rance, what's yours?"

"Bill." Bill began to lower his revolver.

Dehner's voice became solicitous, a hard-working businessman anxious to please a customer. "So, how can we help you, Bill?"

"I'm new in town. At the Mule Kick last night some jaspers tole me this place has the pertiest waitress in the West. So, I paid money to sleep here last night. Came down to see the perty gal and these chinks say she ain't here." Bill raised his gun and began to swing the barrel between the two Asian men. "I want that perty gal and I want her now!"

Bill was a man whose life had been reduced to desperate fantasies. Feeding into those fantasies might save a few lives. "No problem, Bill," Dehner gushed. "You see, this establishment provides special services for special customers. Just get back up to your room and I'll send along a pretty gal to keep you company. No charge, this will be our way of welcoming you to Grayson."

Confusion blanketed Bill's face. The offer sounded too good to be true but he wanted very much to believe it. "You better not be lyin'!"

"I'm not lying," Dehner lied.

Bill pointed his revolver directly at the detective. "You and me is goin' upstairs together. When you provide me with a gal, then I'll believe ya."

Dehner continued to speak in his relentlessly good-natured voice. "Can't blame a man for being careful. Let's get moving. I know just what girl I have in mind for you."

The gunny looked threateningly at the two Asian men. "Both of ya, stay here." He pointed his gun straight ahead. "If either of ya step through them doors, I'll kill your boss."

"Do what Bill says, fellas," Dehner kept smiling as he spoke. "He's new in town, we have to prove to him what Grayson hospitality is all about."

As the detective walked through the restaurant's double doors, he held one of them open for Bill, who was probably alert to the possibility of his prisoner using one of the doors as a weapon.

"What room are you in?" Dehner asked as they began to walk up the stairway to the second floor.

"206." Bill remained one step behind Dehner. There were ten steps in the stairway, Rance had to act fast.

The detective turned toward Bill and spoke in a lewd whisper. "This filly I have for you, she's got blond hair and she's only fourteen. But don't worry, she's an early bloomer, if you get my drift."

"Where is she now?" Bill began to hurry, he was now on the same step as Dehner.

"Room 201, right at the top of the stairs, you can meet with her right there if you'd like," Rance stopped but Bill's mind was now completely centered on the sensuous delight at the top of the stairs. He moved upwards.

Dehner grabbed Bill's gun arm and twisted it. The gunny yelled in pain as he dropped the weapon. Dehner tightened the grip on his opponent's arm and threw him down the stairs.

Sammy came barging through the double doors as Bill was still bouncing down the steps. When Bill hit the floor and began to get up, Sammy did a fast twirl and kicked the gunny in his head.

As he hurried down the stairs Dehner admired Sammy's work. "Nice kick, but don't kick him again. I want Bill to be able to get on his horse and leave town."

"Sammy enjoy himself," the hotel owner proclaimed. "Most the time, Sammy have to be polite to very impolite people, that is what is called the cost of doing business. This morning Sammy express true feelings with foot, that good for the soul."

Dehner helped Bill to his feet. "We're escorting you to your horse and waving good-bye as you leave town, don't come back or you'll go to jail."

"Want my gun," Bill's words were muddled. "Just bought . . . last week . . ."

"Yes, Sammy notice fine weapon!" Sarcasm tinged Sammy's voice. "I keep and sell, use money to pay for damage you just made. Now, we are even, you no need have guilty conscience."

Bill was not cheered, but didn't resist as he was led to his horse. As Dehner had promised both he and the hotel owner waved as Bill, his body hunched over, rode out of town.

"That ungrateful jasper didn't wave back," Dehner proclaimed in mock outrage as Bill slowly vanished. "After all, I could have locked him up."

"Sammy could quote Confucius, be wise but inscrutable Oriental but I skip it if you OK, yes?"

"I'll manage without it," Dehner said as the two men made their way back to the hotel. "You prefer to stay away from Confucius?"

Sammy nodded and smiled. "Many people have ideas of what Chinese are like. I like to surprise them. Sammy dress like ranch hand. No pigtail, too."

"Do you really have a pretty waitress working

for you?" Dehner posed the question as they reentered the hotel.

"Yes, daughter Jenny manage kitchen and help out with hotel. Daughter now away visit family, return on Monday."

Sammy scooted behind the registration desk, grabbed the "Back Soon" sign and placed it under the counter. "Last night when you register you tell Sammy you are detective. Will you be trying to find person responsible for attempting to kill Reverend Colt, ah, please excuse, Reverend Paul Colten?"

"Yes, I'm helping Ox Bently."

"Ox Bently good man, very nice to Sammy and daughter even when not so nice."

"I don't follow you," Dehner said.

"Sammy's restaurant used to have arrangement with town. Restaurant provide food for prisoners in the jail. No more."

"What happened?"

"One day, Ox Bently speak privately with humble self." The hotel owner chortled over his use of humble self. "Ox tell Sammy he do fine job with provide food for prisoners but he could tell Miss Lolly Farnum in tight money situation. So, he give job of feeding jail birds to Miss Lolly."

Sammy laughed loudly and slapped the counter. It appeared to be an action he performed frequently. "Ox Bently good man but act like shy boy around Miss Lolly."

The hotel owner shook his head in amusement. "Confucius have a lot to say about that too, but I say best, just skip it."

The next few days passed quickly as Dehner focused on learning all he could about Grayson and failing to pick up any clues as to who was trying to kill Paul Colten. On Sunday morning the detective did establish that Sammy was right about Ox Bently being a shy boy around Lolly Farnum. Ox arrived early at the church; when Lolly came in the door, he casually strolled over to her and began a conversation. The two then sat together during the service.

Several hours later, the same process was repeated at the evening service. Ox would casually approach Lolly and begin a conversation. The couple would end up sitting together as if it had all transpired without any prior thought. Dehner wondered how long all of this had been going on and how long it would last. Both Ox and Lolly appeared unaware of the amused smirks from other folks in the congregation who were enjoying the weekly performance.

But the detective took his mind off of Ox's awkward courtship techniques and focused on Paul Colten, his sermon and his stamina as he delivered his second sermon of the day. The preacher's vitality was apparent as he ended his message on a personal note. "Doctor Cranston has told me my sling can come off tomorrow. But he doesn't know if I will regain complete use of my right arm. As most of you know, I have used this right arm over the last couple of years in ways I am not proud of. But you people have been kind enough to allow me to return to the call God gave me when I was a very young man. So, whatever the fate of my right arm I intend to serve you and our Lord as best I can."

Clusters of well-wishers gathered around the pastor after the service. Ox and Dehner were among the last ones to leave. They felt a need to once again warn the preacher that he was in danger.

"Rance and me is tryin' hard to find the snake that wants ya dead," Ox explained. "But so far we ain't done nothin' we can brag on."

The sheriff continued in this vein with Rance standing by, nodding in an apologetic manner. Lolly mercifully intervened, "Shut up you two, Paul already knows how worthless you both are!"

Alone in the sanctuary, Paul Colten looked around with gratitude. While talking with the sheriff and the detective, he had spotted Lolly straightening the place up. The hymnals were all back in the racks and the owner of Lolly's Fine Eats had even run outside and returned a couple of handbags to the women who had left them in the pews. Yes, he still needed to grab a broom and sweep the rough wooden floor but that could wait until morning.

The preacher was exhausted. The energy exhibited in the pulpit had been to some degree a show. He almost staggered to the front pew of the church and sat down. He mused to himself that, all jokes aside, the wooden pew was comfortable. Yes, it felt very comfortable.

Colten awoke to the sound of an intruder moving about the church. Instinctively, he began to reach for his gun only to remember his right arm was in a sling and he wasn't carrying a weapon.

Colten realized he was now lying down on the pew. A flickering red light cascaded against the ceiling and he could hear repeating pops of fire. He lurched onto his feet.

A figure in a black robe with a large hood covering its head stood at the opposite end of the church. The figure held a large torch spewing flames and spoke in a sharp whisper that sounded almost like a hiss. "Hell has invaded your sanctuary."

Colten snapped a reply. "What does Hell want with me?"

"Your life. Your soul."

Paul stepped toward the figure which immediately moved the torch in the direction of a back pew. The pastor retreated to his original position. He would have to give up on seeing the strange intruder's face. "Just how do you intend to claim my life and soul?"

The hooded apparition spoke once again in a hiss but a new intensity filled its voice. "Suicide!" The figure turned and quickly walked out of the church. Paul Colten began to run in pursuit but stumbled and slammed against the floor. Pain scorched through his upper body. With his good arm he grabbed onto a pew, pulled himself up and ran outside.

He looked for flames but saw only the total darkness of night. No lights emanated from any-where in Grayson. "I must have slept for hours," Colten whispered to himself. "It looks like two or three in the morning."

Paul looked upward at a starless sky. A moon struggled to cast down light through a moving stampede of clouds. The moon became a blur as did the trees near the church. Colten dropped to the ground.

Chapter Seven

Paul Colten nervously ran an index finger across his thick, light brown mustache as he looked at the two men sitting near one corner of his desk. "Ox, Rance, thanks for coming." He shifted his gaze to the opposite corner. "Scoop and Mandy, I have a favour to ask. You know this town and the people in it. But I'd like for what I'm about to tell you to stay out of the newspaper . . . for a while."

Scoop and Mandy nodded their heads and, along with the sheriff and his volunteer deputy, waited for Colten to collect his thoughts. Dehner noted that the pastor's office they were sitting in at the Grayson Community Church contained a cot. The town's preacher, like the town's sheriff, slept in his office.

Paul rested his hands on the desk and told his visitors what had happened to him the night before. "I woke up early this morning, lying in front of the church." He tossed a stringy, cloth item at Ox. "That was lying beside me."

Ox crunched his face. "Looks like somethin' for a kid. A toy snake 'bout half a foot long with a silly smile on the snake's face." The sheriff gave Paul a smirk. "And the dern thing is red. I ain't never seen a bright, completely red snake."

Colten wasn't amused. "Red is the color most people associate with Hell and the devil." He looked directly at Dehner. "Before he died, didn't Kid Madero say something to you about Satan?"

"Yes. Madero said you were going to die in a slow, awful way, and said the name of Satan twice." Dehner grinned in a cynical manner. "He died himself before he had a chance to elaborate."

Colten pointed at the red item in Ox's hand. "Many people believe Satan's first appearance in the Bible comes in the creation story where he takes on the form of a serpent, or snake."

"True enough," Ox agreed. "But what's that got ta do with anythin'?"

Colten's reply came quick. "I've killed five people over the last two years and sent even more to jail. The way I see it, someone wants vengeance and he's turned to a group of Satanists or become a Satanist himself. He seeks revenge that goes beyond a killing. The first plan of Kid Madero putting me through a night of torment failed, so now he wants to make my life hell on earth and drive me to suicide."

Bently's eyebrows shot up. "How's he gonna do that!"

"By harming people who are important to me, by slowly destroying this town; I'd be driven to kill myself in order to save—"

"A pastor preaches almost every Sunday about a man who gave his life for others," Mandy said.

"Someone must figure you can be pushed to practice what you preach."

Despite the circumstances, Colten managed a smile. "Yes, that seems to be it."

"I know nothing about Satanism," Dehner confessed. "Could you give us some background, Paul?"

"Not very much, I'm afraid. In the big eastern cities, you'll find Satanic temples where Satan worshipers meet on a regular basis. As long as they do nothing illegal the law leaves them alone."

Ox looked dumbfounded. "Why would anyone wanna worship the devil?"

"Power," Colten answered. "Satanists believe if you worship the devil he will give you the power to get what you want."

Dehner tugged on his ear. "In a town the size of Grayson we're probably dealing with just one Satanist. That may have been the person who visited you last night, Paul. Maybe our devil worshiper has one or two accomplices but no more."

"Sounds likely," Bently agreed. "If lots of folks was gatherin' every week to worship old Beelzebub ya can bet I'd take notice."

Rance continued: "Whoever it is, he hired Kid Madero and his pals to carry out the devil's work. We're likely to see another gang of thugs soon."

"Could you give me a list of the men you

have killed," Scoop asked the pastor. "I might be able to establish a connection with one of the townspeople."

"Sure," Colten answered. "But the men I brought down weren't too conscientious about using their correct handle. I killed one owlhoot who called himself Tuscon. That was the name he was buried with, no last name and there's a good chance he had never even been to Tuscon. Outlaws give themselves nicknames that, they hope, confuse the law."

"Lordy," Ox sighed deeply. "Zeke Talbot starts work today . . ."

Scoop looked quizzical. "Isn't he the new deputy you're going to train to become sheriff?"

"Yeh, thought I could start off showin' him how to handle drunks and petty crooks. Looks like he's gonna havta take on the devil hisself." Bently wiggled the toy snake in his hand. "Maybe this will give him a few laughs."

Paul Colten's voice became a soft whisper. "I'm afraid we are going to be seeing more of those toy snakes and there won't be anything funny about it."

Chapter Eight

Cactus Olsen's body moved with the bumps as he pretended to be guiding the stagecoach into Grayson. In fact, the nags had made this trip many times before and needed no direction from the jehu.

"Now, are you sure you wanna be a lawman, boy?" He spoke to his shotgun who sat beside him on the coach's seat. "It's a right thankless job!"

Zeke Talbot didn't immediately reply. The kid probably didn't even hear me, Cactus thought. His mind is on that pretty little filly in the coach. Jenny Wong was returning home after visiting relatives in Houston.

"A lawman's job ain't so bad," Talbot eventually answered as he lifted his Stetson and ran a hand through his sandy hair. "Grayson's my home and I'll get to know the folks there better."

Cactus grimaced. He knew just which one of the folks Zeke wanted to get to know better. Cactus Olsen regretted being so snarky with the boy because he had questioned the truthfulness of his war stories. Given the way young bucks were these days, Zeke's replacement would probably be even more cantankerous. Besides, Cactus conceded silently, maybe he had exaggerated with those stories just a tad.

"Pull up!" Zeke shouted.

Cactus obeyed. Beside the trail was a small hill lined with trees. A cottonwood had apparently tumbled over and now lay across the trail a few yards from the stagecoach.

"We had us a hard rain last week," Cactus spoke as he carefully eyed the fallen tree. "The cottonwood mighta dropped by itself."

Zeke sounded skeptical. "Maybe. We gotta investigate careful like."

Olsen made a guttural sound, acknowledging agreement. The jehu grabbed a rifle from behind the seat and crawled onto the top of the stagecoach. Going by the rules, he should have laid flat on the top of the coach. But he propped up on one knee giving himself a better view of the hill. Cactus's eyes weren't as sharp as they once were.

Winchester in hand, Zeke jumped from the coach and approached a passenger window. "Sorry 'bout this, ma'am," he said to the one passenger. "But we got a tree blocking the road up ahead."

"I appreciate you and Mister Olsen removing the tree. Please let me know if I can be of any assistance."

The woman's voice is a song, Zeke thought. Jenny's oval face conveyed even more music: long black hair, brown eyes and a small mouth that always seemed to be smiling.

"We don't need help, ma'am, but you see, puttin' a tree across the road is an old trick crooks use to hold up a stage. I'm gonna take a look see. It'd be smart for you to crouch down 'til we give you an all-clear, jus' to be safe."

"Yes, of course, and please both you and Mr. Olsen be very careful."

Zeke touched two fingers to his hat and stumbled as he headed toward the hill.

Jenny dropped to her knees and remained in a crouch. She wasn't scared. Twelve of her eighteen years had been spent in the West. China was an increasingly vague memory. She felt grateful to her family for helping her adjust to this new land. For a moment her thoughts turned to Zeke Talbot. What kind of family did he come from?

Gunfire shattered Jenny's thoughts. She heard Cactus screech in pain, curse and fire his rifle. A fast volley of shots followed and then the body of Cactus Olsen created a blur in the passenger window as it plunged to the ground.

Jenny jumped from the coach and knelt over Cactus. She ripped open his shirt and pressed a handkerchief over one of his wounds. "Mr. Olsen, can you hear me?"

Cactus's voice was weak. "Where's my Remington?"

Jenny pointed to the object lying a few feet away, "Over there."

Olsen's speech was becoming broken. "Grab rifle, git back in the coach, if any one tries . . . shoot him."

"No. I will stay with you, Mr. Olsen. We must stop the bleeding and then we will get you into Grayson where Doctor Cranston can attend to you."

"Too late for that, Miss Wong. You've already wasted a pretty 'kerchief on me. Do what I tell ya." A sudden serenity flooded the jehu's eyes. "Guess that pretty face of yours is the last thing I'm gonna see on this earth. Sure, can't complain . . ." His eyes closed.

"Mister Olsen, Mister Olsen!" There was no reply. Jenny began to cry.

A harsh voice cut the air. "This ain't no time for tears, lady. Git up slow like and don't even look at that Remington."

Four men carrying guns approached her. Zeke Talbot, his arms in the air was marching in front of them. As Jenny obeyed the order she had been given, she tried to spot anything unusual about the four gunmen. Something she could pass on to Ox Bently. But the four were wearing red hoods over their heads with spaces cut out for eyes and mouths. All Jenny could spot was mouths which were tobacco stained and ugly.

The outlaw who had spoken and appeared to be the boss pushed Zeke in her direction. She had to step to one side to avoid a collision.

"Sorry, ma'am, but—"

"This is not your fault, Mr. Talbot," Jenny whispered. "We are in the hands of vicious killers and we must obey them."

The boss man spoke again. "OK, boys, you know what to do."

One outlaw ran up the hill while another ascended the stagecoach and tossed down a strongbox. With one shot the leader blew the lock off the box. He kept a gun pointed at Zeke and Jenny as his two companions grabbed packets of bills. Hoofbeats sounded from the hill as the outlaw who had run off returned on horseback leading three other horses. The money was stuffed into saddlebags and all four outlaws quickly mounted.

Jenny noted that the process had been carried out with speed and even looked graceful. These men were monsters but they weren't amateurs.

The foursome looked ready to ride off when the gang member who had gone for the horses rode his steed in Jenny's direction and gave a loud whistle. "This is one good lookin' woman, boss. What say we take her along with us?"

Zeke stood in front of the woman. "You'll have to kill me first."

The thug yanked his pistol from its holster, "Happy to oblige."

The boss man gave a loud shout as he rode toward Zeke and Jenny. "Put that damn thing away, fool!" The leader reined up, reached into his shirt pocket and tossed an object to Jenny. "Kindly give that to Reverend Colt."

As the gang rode off, Jenny stared curiously at the toy red snake in her hand.

Chapter Nine

"Tomorrow I'll be doing the funeral service for Cactus Olsen," Paul Colten spoke half to himself and half to his companions. "It will be the second funeral I've done in less than a week."

"There may be more, Pastor," Rance Dehner said.

Four other people were gathered with Paul Colten in the kerosene yellow of the *Grayson Herald* office: Mandy and Scoop Wilsey, Ox, and Zeke Talbot.

All of those in the office were emotionally spent and seeking the comfort of each other's company. Zeke couldn't sit down, he paced about the office, "I shoulda been more careful . . . don't know how them killers got the drop on me."

"Ya learned an important lesson 'bout bein' a lawdog today, boy." Ox tried to sound harsh but couldn't quite pull it off. "Things don't always go well and when they don't it's plenty hard to swallow."

Scoop turned his gaze to Paul Colten. "How well did you know Cactus Olsen?"

The question seemed to disturb Colten. He paused before answering. "I liked Cactus. He helped with building the church. The man was a jehu, he was gone a lot but we still got to be friends."

Scoop folded his arms and leaned against a wall. "That red snake one of the thugs gave Jenny, connects Cactus's murder to that weird character who visited you in the church yesterday, Paul. You were right, someone is trying to kill off people who are close to you."

"Let's not forget, the stagecoach was carrying a thousand dollars in cash," Dehner added.

Ox agreed with the detective's point. "One thousand dollars: the stage carries a lot more sometimes but usually it don't carry anywheres near a thousand. Them owlhoots either knowed 'bout it or were darned lucky."

"The robbery gives me a strong connection to what's happening in Grayson."

"What do you mean, Rance?" While posing the question, Mandy petted the small dog lying in her lap. Clyde's bandages were now off.

"Kid Madero's dying words were that another group of thugs would be hired to torture Reverend Colt, I mean, Paul Colten. I think there's a good chance at least one of those thugs is an outlaw the Lowrie Detective Agency has a standing contract on."

Mandy's voice made her response a question. "And now you are sure?"

"I'll bet the Lowrie Agency and our competition has already received telegrams from Wells Fargo promising big rewards for the capture or killing of those involved in today's hold-up and murder and, of course, the return of the money."

Mandy's husband continued with the questioning. "So, what are you going to do?"

"First thing in the morning I'm sending another telegram to my boss, telling him I'm after Cactus's killers and will try to recover the money. I will tell him all I know about the case and send along that list of men Paul killed when he was a gunfighter. That may help us find who is orchestrating all of this. It almost has to be someone living in Grayson."

Everyone in the room nodded their heads or made facial gestures acknowledging agreement with what Dehner had said. A brief period of quiet followed which Scoop broke. "Paul, the killing of Cactus Olsen following so quick on Sally Ward's murder has this whole town spooked. People are saying a lot of crazy things."

The clergyman agreed. "Yes, I've heard some of those crazy things."

"We need to print the truth, all of the truth, as best we know it." Scoop pressed on, "As you know, the paper comes out on Wednesday and Saturday. For the Wednesday edition, I want to go with the story of your weird Sunday night visitor, including all of the Satan stuff, red snakes and all."

Anxiety shot across Colten's face. Scoop

wouldn't retreat. "The truth is our best tool. Without it, people will cook up monsters far worse than Kid Madero."

Paul sighed deeply. "You're right . . . print the whole story."

Mandy spoke quietly, responding to Paul's dismay. "I don't think most of our readers will take the Satan stuff seriously. They'll know someone is just blowing smoke."

"You're wrong, Mandy," Colten's voice was polite but firm. "We're dealing with someone who believes in the power of Satan and is trying to use that power against me and making me a threat to this whole town."

Chapter Ten

After the meeting, the Wilseys returned to their home and Paul Colten to the church, leaving Dehner alone with the two lawmen on the boardwalk outside of the newspaper office.

"Go home and git some rest, Zeke," Ox instructed. "Rance and I kin look after the town tonight."

Zeke thanked his companions and hurried off, not to the boarding house where he lived, but to Sammy's Hotel and Restaurant. As the deputy stepped into the lobby he wondered if he could continue to eat there often. Ox seemed to be keeping company a lot with Lolly Farnum. The sheriff might look down on his deputy patronizing the competition for Lolly's Fine Eats.

"Ox is only gonna be sheriff for a few weeks, 'til I get trained," Zeke mumbled to himself. "I'll eat where I please."

Sammy Wong looked amused as he bustled about behind the hotel's counter. Sammy frequently looked amused. The man had boundless energy.

"Good evening, Sammy!"

Sammy paused and bowed. "Good evening, great honour to welcome esteemed Deputy Sheriff to my unworthy establishment."

The hotel owner slapped the top of his desk and laughed. "Please excuse, just have two people from out of town arrive. Out of towners confused by Sammy. He Chinese but not act as Americans think of Chinese."

"It ain't jus' visitors, Sammy, you also got the locals confused plenty."

"Even confuse daughter, Sammy tell daughter to call him father, not honourable father."

"Why?"

"Ox Bently tell Sammy that man who brag about being tough, not tough. Really tough man have no need to tell people he tough. Same thing go for honourable man, you think yes?"

"Guess so. Ah, speaking of your daughter . . ."

Sammy pointed to his left. "She still working but business slow, have time to talk." Sammy paused and then laughed once again. "Daughter always have time to talk."

Zeke gave the establishment owner a quick thanks and made his way through the double doors. There were only two other customers in the restaurant at this late hour: Harold Cogan, the town's banker and his wife, Sylvia. They were sitting in front of plates empty except for crumbs. Jenny was pouring them what was obviously not their first cup of coffee.

Seeing Zeke seat himself, Jenny hurriedly returned the coffee pot to the kitchen and then approached his table. "Good evening."

"Good evenin'."

I'm talking too loud, he admonished himself as he dropped his voice. "Things don't look too busy."

"Most of our supper customers have gone," the woman's voice was music as always Zeke thought, but she did sound like she was speaking to a child. "Mr. and Mrs. Cogan frequently eat late because Mr. Cogan work late." Jenny shifted her eyes toward her other customers. "People who make joke about banker's hours know not of what they speak."

The Cogans laughed heartily. "You tell 'em, young lady," Harold shouted.

Zeke cringed. Jenny was paying more attention to the Cogans than she was to him. He needed to try harder. "I hope you're over ever'thing that happened today."

"My heart still breaks for Mr. Olsen."

"Yeh, sure, I feel the same." Zeke prattled aimlessly for a few minutes about the friendship he had with Cactus Olsen, while he silently chastised himself. This wasn't the way things were supposed to go. He and Jenny had been through bad times that morning. They should be comforting each other.

When the deputy was finished babbling, Jenny said something polite and then ended with, "What can I bring for you tonight?"

"Ah, pie and coffee."

"Apple or cherry?"

"Ah, apple . . . please."

While Zeke waited for his food, the Cogans left the restaurant. As they passed by his table, Harold gave him a wink as if wishing him good luck. "Damn, am I that obvious?" the deputy whispered to himself.

As Jenny placed his pie and coffee on the table, he asked her to sit down and join him, "Jus' for a few minutes."

The lady looked uncomfortable but complied. Zeke fiddled with his fork before speaking. "You know, I'm a deputy now, I'll soon be the sheriff."

Jenny smiled but said nothing.

"You're gonna be seein' a lot more of me around town and at this restaurant," the deputy said buoyantly. "You know, Sammy's Hotel and Restaurant is part of our daily patrols."

The lady's voice was still music but not buoyant. "A lawman's job is very hard, more so because of the murders of Mr. Olsen and Mrs. Ward. My father and I will be praying for you."

Zeke fell silent. He had not anticipated the spiritual direction the conversation was taking.

"Please excuse," Jenny said. "Hoa, our cook, needs me in the kitchen."

The new deputy gulped his pie and coffee,

paid for the food and left feeling that his stop at Sammy's Hotel and Restaurant had been a failure. "What did I do wrong," he mumbled to a dark sky. There was no answer.

Chapter Eleven

"I hope Zeke gets himself trained real quick," Lolly Farnum said. "Ox Bently's got too much to do with bein' mayor and ownin' half the town. And, what with all these killin's goin' on, doubt if he can handle everything."

Mandy suspected that Lolly's concern for Ox went beyond the acting sheriff having a crammed schedule. "I'm sure Zeke is a fast learner. Meanwhile, Ox has Rance Dehner to help him."

Lolly nodded her head but didn't seem to feel any better.

Mandy and Lolly were riding out to the Locke ranch which was about an hour's ride from Grayson. It would be Mandy's final visit and she felt a need for confession. "I want to thank you, Lolly, for suggesting I interview Rebecca. At first, I didn't really think anything would come of it. But 'Rebecca Remembers' is one of the most popular items in the *Grayson Herald*."

The restaurant owner smiled wistfully. "Rebecca and George built their ranch when Grayson weren't much more than a general store and a saloon. She's got a lot of stories to tell, though I reckon she fancies them up a bit."

"Is that really true about Rebecca and George never trusting a bank?"

"Could be," Lolly answered. "Like I said, Rebecca likes to sort of add on to her tales."

"People know Rebecca tosses in a bit of fiction into her stories and don't mind . . . but . . . I didn't print what she told me on our last visit."

Mandy stopped speaking. Rebecca's past was wonderful and exciting but not her present. When her husband had died three years before, Rebecca did a fine job of running the ranch on her own. But the last sixteen months had seen troubling changes. Rebecca was becoming increasingly irrational and confused. During her last interview with Mandy, the woman had been scattered and irrational.

"Rebecca's son is coming . . . tomorrow isn't it . . . to take her to Houston?" Mandy asked.

"Yep," Lolly answered. "The new owners arrive next week. Some of the ladies from the church have been stayin' with Rebecca much as they can, I'll be here for a few hours, but the poor woman is still alone much of the time; good thing her son is takin' her to Houston."

They were approaching the once bustling ranch which now looked barren with an empty barn and corral facing the ranch house. "I wish I could stay longer," the newspaperwoman said, "but I need to get back for Cactus Olsen's funeral and—"

"Don't worry 'bout it none," Lolly replied as both ladies dismounted and tied their horses to a hitch rail in front of the house. "It's really nice you're comin' to say good-bye and pretendin' to git another story—"

A loud scream sounded from inside the house. Both women bolted through the front door. Rebecca Locke, a thin, frail looking woman with stringy gray hair stumbled toward them.

Lolly grabbed the elderly woman before she fell. "Rebecca, what's wrong?"

"Satan! The devil himself, he's in this house!"

"Sit down, Rebecca," Lolly nodded toward a chair. "There's no devil here."

"He's been torturing me all night. I couldn't sleep." Rebecca, wearing a robe, pointed toward her bedroom. "He's in there right now!"

"Could you have a look?" Lolly asked Mandy as she guided the elderly woman toward the chair.

The newspaperwoman approached the bedroom hurriedly but slowed down as she entered. The room was totally dark. The outline of a bed was visible. She could see little else but did hear a hissing sound. Moving toward the bed, Mandy could see something moving on top of it. A loud screech filled the room as a black cat jumped off the bed and ran past her.

The cat scrambled into the living room heading toward Rebecca who was now sitting in a chair. The woman flung her body away from the animal and screamed, "Satan! Satan!"

Mandy silently admitted to herself that the

animal looked demonic. One side of the cat's face was crunched up with a scar running under a half closed eye.

Lolly placed her hands on the frail woman's shoulders and spoke calmly to the newspaper-woman. "Rebecca has always been superstitious, please git that animal outta here."

The task wasn't easy; the cat, frightened by Rebecca's scream, jumped onto the thick curtains that covered a front window. The screaming continued as the feline made its way up the curtains toward the ceiling.

Mandy figured the animal was even more frightened than Rebecca. She opened the front door wide, then waited for the cat to jump back onto the floor. When the animal finally did she shooed it toward the means of escape. When the cat spotted the route to freedom it sprinted out the door which Mandy immediately closed.

Rebecca's screaming morphed into a low cry. Lolly tried to be of comfort. "There's nothin' to be upset 'bout, jus' a stray cat that somehow got into your house."

"Satan, Satan," the elderly woman's voice was weak, in a few moments her eyes closed and her head dropped into sleep.

"Poor woman," Lolly said. "I think she was tellin' the truth 'bout not gittin' much shut eye last night. That danged cat scared her somethin' awful."

Confusion covered Mandy's face. "When I was here last time, Rebecca kept talking about demons, Satan and such."

Lolly lifted the woman from her chair. "Could you give me a hand? I'm gonna put her back in bed."

Lolly carried Rebecca to her bedroom and Mandy smoothed the covers on the bed and helped ensure that the woman was comfortable. As the two women returned to the living room, Mandy's voice took on a slightly guilty tinge. "There's really not any more I can do, guess I'll get back to town."

"Don't feel bad, I can keep that danged cat outta the house all by myself."

As she rode back to Grayson, Mandy thought about her father who had died several months before. She missed him every day. And yet, she felt gratitude for the fact that up until the moment he died from a heart attack, Joseph Woods was a healthy vigorous man who served as sheriff of Grayson, a job he loved. Seeing Rebecca the way she was now . . .

Gunshots exploded Mandy's thoughts. She reined up and looked backwards. Smoke was coming from the Locke ranch. The woman reckoned she had been riding for about fifteen minutes. She kneed her pinto into a gallop back to the Locke's place.

The horse slowed and began to neigh in protest

as they got onto the ranch and close to the flames which engulfed the house. Smoke was becoming thick and Mandy could hear the panicked nattering of another horse. Lolly appeared riding out from a dark billowing stream of gray. Unsteady hands held the reins of her horse. She swayed in the saddle as she pulled up.

"Lolly—you're hurt!"

"I kin make it."

"Where's Rebecca?"

"Dead. They killed her . . . it was awful . . . they've gone now . . ."

"Who—" Mandy grabbed her friend's shoulder and stabilized her position in the saddle. The newspaperwoman coughed and her eyes teared up from the smoke which was now enveloping them. "Hold onto to the horn of your saddle, Lolly. We have to get out of here!"

Both horses bucked, almost in unison. Mandy grabbed the reins of Lolly's chestnut with one hand while keeping a tight grip on the reins of her pinto with the other. As they rode off from the fire the steeds calmed.

Away from the smoke, Mandy could see bruises on the side of Lolly's head. Her friend was fighting to remain conscious. This was not the time for questions.

A scrambling sound came from below. Mandy glanced downward. The black cat was following them into town.

Chapter Twelve

"Keep the ice pressed against your noggin', Lolly," Doctor Cranston ordered. "The bruise ain't bad. That rock hard head of yours will be back to normal in a day or so."

Lolly's response also had the sound of an order. "Thanks a lot, Doc, now go peddle your pills."

Ox Bently chimed in. "Before ya do anythin' else, Doc, stop by the place where ya got the ice. Tell 'em Ox is settin' you up."

"Thank you, Ox, I think a visit to the Mule Kick is a great idea. And later on I'll drop in to Lolly's Fine Eats and enjoy a free dinner."

Lolly's voice took on force. "Only one piece of pie for dessert, Fred Cranston, you—"

Doctor Cranston laughed as he exited the sheriff's office. Besides his patient, the doctor left behind Ox, Zeke Talbot, Rance Dehner, both of the Wilseys and Reverend Colt. The sheriff's voice took on an uncharacteristically soft tone. "Mandy has tole us ever thin' she can 'bout what happened, Lolly. You feel up to talkin' now?"

"Of course I do!" The bravado quickly left the restaurant owner's voice. Her eyes shifted to the door as if wishing Fred Cranston were still around to do more harmless battle.

Ox prodded with a quiet question. "How long after Mandy left did the trouble start?"

"Couldn't been more than a few minutes, suddenly some jasper wearin' a red hood seemed to appear from outta nowhere carryin' a gun. He opened the front door, shouted somethin' and three other men came in."

"And they also wore red hoods?" Dehner asked.

"Yes."

Dehner faced the sheriff and spoke quickly. "Four hooded men, probably the same bunch that robbed the stagecoach and killed the driver."

Ox nodded agreement but kept his eyes on Lolly. "Tell us best ya can, what happened."

"One of them hardcases pushed me aside, stalked right into the bedroom, then pulled out a knife and held it under Rebecca's chin. Started tellin' her how he was gonna cut her up real slow like. He terrified the old woman, and she started screamin'. I couldn't take no more. I ran at that buzzard, but I didn't help Rebecca none. Somethin' hard hit me in the side of the head and I went down, good for nothin'."

"Were you unconscious for a while?" Dehner asked.

"No, almost wish I was. When I looked up I saw that thug plunging his knife into Rebecca, makin' it as painful for her as he could, it was hell . . . the blood, the helpless cryin' out . . ."

"Ya don't have ta talk about that no more,

Lolly," Ox said. "Tell us what happened after Rebecca was killed."

"They took me outside and put me on my horse." She reached into her pocket and pulled out a familiar toy. "They tole me to give this to Reverend Colt with a message."

Paul Colten took a few steps toward Lolly and carefully took the item from her. He stared for a moment at the red snake, its silly smile appeared to be mocking him. The pastor's voice was barely a whisper. "What was the message?"

Lolly's lips trembled, she looked downwards for a moment then lifted her head. "Satan doesn't need darkness. He strikes in sunshine too."

Colten's face turned ashen. He squeezed the red object in his right hand as if trying to destroy it. When he opened his fist the snake was still smirking at him.

Paul Colten was a tormented man and, for the moment, there was no help for it. The sheriff continued to question Lolly. "Tell us what happened after the outlaws put you on your horse."

"It's all sort of a blur, maybe I did pass out for a minute or two. I remember hearin' gunshots and horses ridin' off. Then there was smoke all 'round and my horse started kickin' up. I rode away from the house and then, thank God, Mandy came along."

Ox Bently looked out the window of his office at the shreds of sunlight making a faint impression on the boardwalk. "It's getting dark. I'll have ta wait 'til mornin' before I kin ride out to the Locke place and find poor Rebecca's body. Hope the hot cinders keep the coyotes away from her."

"I'll talk with her son, who's due in town tomorrow," Paul Colten said. "And I'll arrange for Rebecca's funeral. I seem to be getting very good at giving eulogies."

Still clasping the red snake in his hand, Colten left the office. Mandy started after him but her husband stopped her.

"Let him go," Scoop advised. "Paul needs some time to be alone with God."

"You're right," Mandy conceded, "only . . ." She paused as if not wanting to say what was on her mind but feeling it necessary. "I hope that will be enough."

Chapter Thirteen

Lolly Farnum poured her only customers' second cups of coffee. "Guess you two expect special treatment 'cause you're my first customers, well, it's time you stopped fiddlin' around and got busy . . ." She stopped, remembering what lay ahead for the two men.

Ox shook his head and watched Lolly return to the kitchen. "She got dragged through the fires of Hell yesterday. Lolly shoulda took the day off. But maybe workin' is better."

The sheriff took a long sip of java then watched his reflection slosh about in the cup. "Obliged to ya for goin' out to the Locke place with me this mornin', Rance. I think it good to let Zeke be in charge of the town for a while."

The detective drank his coffee and smiled appreciatively at the brew. "There are some things I want to look into at the Locke place."

Both men rose from the table, placed some money on it, then headed for the door where a reedy bald headed man was entering. "Hello, Jared," Ox was obviously surprised to see Jared Ward. "What brings ya into town?"

Ward understood the real question. "I gotta keep busy, Ox. After what happened to Sally, well . . . I need to see Harold Cogan, the banker on some routine business, buy some supplies and just keep moving. Reckon I'll talk with Reverend Colt some, only I don't think he wants to be called that no more."

"Paul Colten is a pretty easy fella, he'll let ya call him anythin' ya want."

Ox's joke was forced but Jared appreciated the effort. He nodded good-bye to the two men then headed for a table. He began to pull out a chair for his wife to sit beside him, then realizing that gesture was no longer necessary, he sat down alone.

Ox and Rance located Rebecca Locke's body quickly. They wrapped her in blankets, placed the corpse on the bed of a buckboard and began to examine the burnt wreckage of what had been the Locke ranch house. Dehner's attention went to a black singed desk which laid flat on its back.

"Ox, take a look at this."

Ox quickly approached Dehner, a cautious hope filled his voice. "Find somethin'?"

The detective pointed downward. "Have you seen this desk before?"

"Don't reckon I have. George and Rebecca were friendly folks. I've visited here many times but never went into George's office . . . no reason to, I suppose."

"Look at the bottom right of the desk."

Ox's eyes took on a new intensity, "Someone

has been at that desk with an ax . . . and they done it recent."

"The roof and frame of this house are ashes, but this desk is heavy, it probably didn't get knocked over in the fire. Before putting a match to this house the thugs knocked the desk over and chopped open the bottom drawer. They thought the flames would destroy any evidence of their work."

Bently pressed his lips together before speaking. "Ever'one knew the story 'bout George and Rebecca not trustin' the bank."

"With all this talk about red snakes and black cats we need to keep two things in mind," Rance asserted. "One thousand dollars was stolen in a stagecoach hold-up and now the desk where the Lockes may have kept a large stash of money has been smashed open."

Ox Bently glanced at the surrounding destruction. "The devil may be at work but he ain't workin' for nothin'."

Chapter Fourteen

Scoop Wilsey placed a stack of newspapers on the registration desk of Sammy's Hotel and Restaurant. He then handed the owner a free copy of the *Grayson Herald*.

"I sure appreciate you selling the papers for me, Sammy," Scoop said.

"Sammy is only upholding the wisdom of Mr. Thomas Jefferson, 'Whenever the people are informed, they can be trusted with their own government.'"

Scoop was genuinely impressed. "That's wonderful, Sammy, you being able to quote Thomas Jefferson."

The hotel owner shrugged. "Not so wonderful. Sammy spend a lot of time behind this desk and reads books. But quoting Mr. Jefferson camouflages real reason for selling the *Grayson Herald*."

"And that is?"

"People come into town on Wednesday night for prayer meeting. Often, eat in town, before attend meeting. Lolly Farnum sell newspaper at her restaurant. Sammy must keep up with competition."

"Suppose so . . ."

"Many store owners sell paper for similar reason. People come into store to buy paper often end up buying something else. In famous words, 'When all is said and done it always come down to dollar.' "

"Who said that?" Scoop asked.

"Don't know, but very wise man."

Scoop nodded, said he would be back tomorrow to pick up the money and left. Outside, he looked about contentedly. Sammy's Hotel and Restaurant was his last stop in distributing the paper to all the businesses that sold it and already he had heard people talking about the stories regarding the murders of Sally Ward, Cactus Olsen and Rebecca Locke. Keeping with their policy of printing the whole truth, Mandy and Scoop had included a mention of the strange late night visitor Paul Colten had encountered at the church.

Scoop mounted his horse with its now empty saddlebags. Scoop Wilsey was not hard hearted. He grieved the loss of life and the violence which threatened the community. But he had a journalist's sense that the *Grayson Herald* was providing a vital service and was at the very heart of what was going on in the town and that gave him a strong feeling of satisfaction.

He tied up his black in front of the *Grayson Herald* office as he nodded at folks coming out the door with recently purchased papers. Stepping inside, he saw his wife carefully arranging a dwindling number of newspapers.

"Are all the papers distributed?" she asked.

"Yep!"

"Good!" The woman closed her eyes and inhaled deeply before speaking. "We've almost sold out of the copies we have here. I think all of the editions will be gone before the prayer meeting tonight."

Scoop pointed at the remaining papers. "As soon as those things are sold, let's close up. We'll eat at Sammy's. That will give us some time to, ah, relax before the meeting starts." Satisfaction was not Scoop's only strong feeling.

"And how exactly do you plan on relaxing?" Mandy's reply was playful. Scoop was encouraged.

The front door banged open, shattering Scoop's encouragement. Jared Ward almost stumbled inside. His face was red and he was waving a copy of the newspaper in his hand, "Why didn't you tell about them?!"

Scoop shrugged in confusion. "What do you mean?"

"The people who killed my wife, then slaughtered Cactus and Rebecca, the Satan worshipers, why didn't you tell who they was?"

Ward's entire body trembled, his face was red and he seemed unsteady on his feet. Mandy gently took the rancher's arm and guided him toward a chair. "Please, Mr. Ward, sit down."

Jared Ward complied but a vicious hatred flared

from his eyes, as he looked up at Scoop Wilsey. "Well, answer my question, why don't you tell who them Satanists are?"

Both Wilseys noticed a whiff of alcohol on Ward's breath. He was a man who usually didn't drink much. Scoop spoke in a soft monotone. "I don't know who the Satanists are, Mr. Ward, nobody does."

"Damn fools!" the rancher shouted. "Look around you, we only got two slant eyes in this here town, Sammy Wong and that daughter of his—"

Scoop could only manage a "What?!"

"Everyone knows them chinks worship all sorts of demons. We get rid of them and the killin' will stop."

Mandy placed a hand on the rancher's shoulder. "Mr. Ward, Sammy and Jenny aren't Satanists. Why, they helped to build the church and they attend every Sunday night."

Ward angrily swiped the woman's hand away. "They won't be attendin' this Sunday. Those slant eyes ain't got the whole town buffaloed like they got youse. We're doin' somethin' about 'em and we're doin' it tonight."

Hands on hips, Scoop looked down at the floor for a moment trying to contain his anger. Jared Ward was an outstanding citizen who had done much for the community. Tragedy had pushed Jared off the edge. The newspaperman tried to bring him back. "Mr. Ward, you're not yourself, you're usually very sensible but grief is making you say—"

The rancher lurched from the chair and pointed an accusing finger at Scoop. "You wouldn't know common sense if it slapped you in the face. But you're gonna learn about it tonight!"

Ward threw his copy of the newspaper onto the floor and spit on it. He walked as quickly as his unsteady gait would allow and exited, slamming the door.

Jared Ward's intrusion had awakened Clyde. The small dog had cautiously made his way from his bed toward his two owners. Mandy bent over to pet the animal while looking at her husband, "I think this means real trouble."

"Folks think highly of Jared, his word carries a lot of weight."

"What are we going to do?"

"Don't know exactly," Scoop answered. "But I'm going to the sheriff's office. Ox will come up with some good ideas . . . I hope!"

Chapter Fifteen

Mandy Wilsey felt nervous and out of place as she stood on the platform of the Grayson Community Church and looked out on a congregation of confused faces. "As all of you can see, I am not our pastor, Paul Colten."

There was a short spurt of polite laughter. People wanted her to get to the explanation.

"Paul Colten is on a very special mission tonight and will be needing our prayers." Mandy's statement was deliberately vague. She recalled what Ox had told her less than an hour before, "Paul is helpin' us protect Sammy and Jenny. He wants you at the church leadin' the meetin'."

Mandy had at first objected. "Wouldn't it be better to just cancel tonight's meeting?"

"No," Ox insisted. "We want most folks off the street and away from trouble. Besides, ya need to put in a good word for us. This may be a long night."

A wave of discontent waved over the congregation. Someone shouted out, "Can't you tell us more?"

Mandy's nervousness increased. She glanced downward and saw that her companion was totally comfortable. Clyde beamed at being in front of so many people.

The newspaperwoman decided to go with the truth; or at least that chunk of the truth Ox had given her permission to share. "Paul is helping Ox Bently, Zeke Talbot, Rance Dehner and my husband with a law enforcement matter that just came up. They need our prayers as we also need to pray for Jared Ward, and the families of all of the people who have been recently murdered."

Mandy's words created tension which exploded into loud screams and shouts as Clyde growled, then barked loudly and ran toward the back of the church. A screech fired over the pandemonium.

Lolly Farnum stood up from a back pew and grabbed Clyde's target before he could get to it. "Ever'one be calm," she shouted. "It ain't nothin' but a cat." She opened the door of the church and tossed the animal outside.

Tail wagging, Clyde returned to his mistress. The newspaperwoman petted the dog, then again addressed the group. "Grayson has gone through some terrible and tragic events, but we must keep our good sense and not get anxious over a cat."

Tom Bascomb, the store owner who had been sitting near Lolly, stood up. "That weren't just any cat, Mandy. Not according to what you wrote."

The newspaperwoman gave Tom a confused look. "What do you mean?"

Bascomb pointed at the door behind him. "That animal Lolly put out, it was a black cat with a scar on its face and one eye almost closed. The cat you wrote about in the paper, the one Rebecca thought was Satan. We might have just been visited by the devil!"

Chapter Sixteen

Rance Dehner left the Mule Kick Saloon and made his way quickly to the sheriff's office. The four men in the office were happy to see him. Waiting is always hard. Dehner had been keeping an eye on the situation at the Mule Kick where Jared Ward was drinking a lot and firing up hatred for the Wongs even more.

"We'd better put your plan into action, Ox," Rance declared. "Ward is getting drunker and crazier by the minute. He's being prodded by a hardcase named Butch, a heavy set jasper, stands at about five and a half feet with a bald spot on top of his head."

"Know anythin' 'bout this Butch character?" Bently asked as Zeke grabbed a Winchester from the rifle rack on the wall, Scoop patted the gun in his shoulder holster as if making sure it was still there and Paul Colten worked his right arm, testing its usefulness.

"No," Dehner admitted.

Bently turned to his deputy. "Get over to Sammy's place, keep an eye on both him and Jenny. I know it'll be hard with Sammy at the desk and his daughter in the restaurant. Do the best ya can. They've been warned to shout if anything suspicious starts happenin'."

"OK," rifle in hand, Zeke almost ran out of the office.

The remaining four men shared a smile. Zeke obviously relished the assignment he had been hinting that he wanted.

"Let's git to the Mule Kick," Bently's statement was close to an order.

As they made their way to the saloon, Rance nervously spoke to Paul Colten. "Are you sure you want to come along? I mean, you're trying to brush off the Reverend Colt reputation and—"

Paul understood his new friend's anxiety. "I need to be there. I couldn't talk Jared out of all this craziness earlier in the day. So, now I have to stop him from doing something he'll regret the rest of his life."

Dehner understood but still felt nervous. Ox Bently's plan was very wide open, that's the only way it could be. They would stay in the Mule Kick and toss cold water on any plans to attack Sammy and his daughter. They wouldn't allow any of the trouble makers to leave the saloon if they planned on heading for the hotel.

How they would execute this plan would be decided on a moment. There could be serious violence and Paul Colten was a man with only partial use of his right arm.

Ox entered the Mule Kick accompanied by his volunteer deputies. The sheriff approached a table, near the bar, where Jared Ward was sitting with the man Dehner identified as Butch. As planned, the deputies scattered throughout the saloon where they could watch everyone.

Ward shouted something about foreigners that got muddled in his slurred speech. Butch placed a hand on Jared's shoulder and yelled out in a clear voice. "Jared Ward is one of the finest men in this here town and his wife got murdered because of some heathen chinks."

Butch pointed a finger at Ox who now stood only a few feet away. "The law won't do nothin'. Ya know why? The law only cares about them rich vultures who run the railroad. They're the ones brought the Chinese over here to build the railroad fer wages no decent man would accept!"

Shouts of agreement blared across the saloon. Jared looked directly at Ox. The hatred which had dominated the rancher's eyes earlier in the day seemed to be morphing into despair. "Why don't you do something? Them Satan worshipers are destroying all of us!"

Ox Bently looked with sympathy at an old friend. "I don't think the Satan folks have to work too hard, Jared. You're doin' a pretty good job of destroyin' yourself."

The sheriff's words quieted the room. Dehner noted a troubled look on Butch's face. The hard-case didn't like the sudden change of mood.

"Say, ain't ya the gunny they call Reverend Colt?" The voice was loud, high pitched and sharp. It came from the opposite end of the saloon from where Jared Ward was sitting.

Dehner spotted a stringy young man of average height walking to where he would be facing Paul Colten from a distance of about ten feet. The Stetson on his head and the Remington hanging under his hip were new. The rest of his clothes were worn and dusty reflecting the life of a ranch hand.

Colten smiled softly at the kid who was challenging him. "Yes, I used to be a gunfighter and I used to be called Reverend Colt. All that is in the past. Why don't you just call me, Paul? And what's your name?"

"People call me Wolf and I'll call ya anything I damn well please."

Scoop Wilsey who was standing near Colten yelled at Wolf. "You coward! You're challenging a man who's been shot and barely has use of his right arm!"

Wolf shrugged his shoulders in an elaborate, mocking manner. "If Reverend Colt wants ta act like a cripple and back down, he kin."

Dehner understood the situation. Wolf was a restless kid hungry for glory. By the time the full story of how he outdrew Reverend Colt got around, he'd already have the reputation he craved.

Both Dehner and Wilsey began to move toward the trouble maker. Colten waved them off. The

116

pastor's voice took on a wistful quality. "I once tried to help a young man like you, Wolf. I failed, I failed horribly."

"Do tell."

"That young man ended up dead."

"You tryin' to make me blubber like a baby, Reverend Colt?"

Colten pushed back the left side of his frock coat revealing a holstered gun. "No, I'm trying to change your life, not end it. The West presents a lot of great opportunities for a young man. Take advantage of them and walk away from foolish dreams."

"Make me walk away!"

Paul Colten said nothing.

"Just like I thought, yore a coward." Keeping an eye on the gun holstered on Colten's hip, Wolf drew his Remington. The .44 was barely out of his holster when a shot exploded from Colten's right hand. Wolf screamed in pain, turned and fought to keep his balance as pain burned through his leg. He clung to the .44.

As Colten ran toward the young man, he used his left hand to grab the Derringer from his right hand. He swung a vicious left hook at his stumbling opponent. The Derringer connected with Wolf's jaw and the kid went down.

Scoop ran toward the pastor, a shocked look on his face. "How—"

Paul showed his friend the small weapon. "I

had this holstered on my wrist. A trick I learned from a gambler. I thought it might come in handy tonight. The gun on my left side was a decoy." He looked down at the figure now groaning on the floor. "I'm sorry it was all necessary."

"It weren't fair!" A short, muscular man who also appeared to be a ranch hand lurched up from the table where Wolf had been sitting. "That was a damned, dirty trick! Wolf didn't stand a chance."

"Sit down, you fool!" Wilsey shouted as he pointed at the gun in Paul's hand. "That Derringer holds two bullets. Your pal could be dead now but the pastor settled for knocking him down."

"No one tells me to sit down!" The short man charged at Scoop Wilsey who stopped him with a hard combination of punches to the head.

Chaos reigned as more of Wolf's fellow ranch hands charged the newspaperman. Ox yelled at the bartender to get Doc Cranston, then ran toward the fray as Dehner approached from a different direction.

Ox fired a bullet into the ceiling. "Calm down, all of ya's!"

The pandemonium didn't stop but it subsided. A couple of men formed a protective barrier around Wolf to ensure he didn't get trampled on.

Dehner suddenly realized he had taken his eyes

off the real trouble. He turned his head to see Jared Ward sitting alone. Butch had left. Dehner ran from the saloon and did a quick turn toward Sammy's Hotel and Restaurant.

Chapter Seventeen

Sounds of painful groans greeted Dehner as he barged into Sammy's establishment. He ran toward the reception desk where the top of the owner's head was visible as he struggled to get on to his feet.

Dehner placed both hands on the desk, preparing to jump it and help the injured man. But Sammy muttered, "Daughter" and pointed toward the doors that led to the restaurant.

Going through the double doors, Dehner saw only a small scattering of customers. All of them looked scared.

"Trouble!" Hoa, the cook, lay on the floor, his head bloodied. He waved in the direction of the kitchen.

The detective charged through the open doorway. Butch was yelling curses as he slammed against the floor. Zeke stood over the outlaw, a look of triumph on his face. Jenny was standing several steps behind the fighters, near a wood-burning range that covered most of the back wall and held a large kettle of soup circled at the bottom by flames. She watched intensely but, otherwise, no emotion showed on her face.

The deputy's Winchester was lying on a counter that ran along most of a side wall that snuggled beside the range. Dehner wondered why Zeke had put it there but didn't have time to speculate.

"I ain't finished with ya yet, ya yella coward!" the deputy shouted as he waved a fist.

The boast was short lived. Butch kicked Zeke's ankle. Talbot screamed in pain as he lifted his injured leg. Butch kicked the deputy's other ankle. Zeke collapsed.

Spotting the new arrival, Butch scrambled to his feet, drew his pistol, took a few steps back and grabbed Jenny. "Stay right where you're at, both of ya's."

Dehner was only a few steps into the kitchen. Zeke was now wobbling on injured ankles facing the outlaw who was a few feet away, one arm enveloping Jenny, the other holding his gun.

Butch's eyes glanced toward the back door on the other side of the oven from the counter. "I'm takin' this girlie and—"

The outlaw screamed as the elbow on his gun arm backed into the flame that circled the kettle. While bellowing, he dropped his gun and let go of Jenny. The young woman bolted out of the kitchen. Butch hastily scooped up the pistol and fired a shot in Rance's direction. But the scorching pain in his arm didn't allow for accuracy. The bullet burrowed into the top of the doorway.

Gun still in hand, Butch barged through the back door. The slight flame crawling up his sleeve went out. Rance followed after him. Zeke started to join the chase but stumbled and fell. Jenny hastened back into the kitchen and helped him up.

Outside, Dehner could hear the outlaw running up the alley between Sammy's place and a barber shop. The detective cautiously followed his .45 in hand. In the darkness of the alley, he could see a bulky shadow move past a boardwalk. Butch appeared to be heading for the hitch rail in front of the hotel.

Dehner reached the break in the boardwalk as Butch, still holding his gun, began to mount his horse. The sorrel apparently smelled the blood now streaming from Butch's arm. The horse bucked as the outlaw tried to pull away from the hitch rail.

The outlaw spotted Dehner, and aimed his gun in the detective's direction. He never pulled the trigger. A red-orange lance from Rance's .45 ripped into Butch's shoulder and he plunged to the ground. The sorrel ran off.

Dehner couldn't make out the words of desperation which spewed from Butch's mouth as, lying in the dirt, he picked up the gun he had dropped in the fall.

"Put it down," Dehner yelled. "Last chance, I—"

A shot cut the air and Butch's head exploded. The detective glanced backward and saw Zeke Talbot lowering the just fired Winchester.

Talbot's walk revealed a limp as he made his way directly to the corpse. Dehner followed behind the deputy, noting that Zeke's eyes never left the dead outlaw. He continued to look at him with a ferocious anger.

"He made me look like a fool back there."

Dehner wasn't sure if the comment had been made to him but tried to answer it anyway. "The important thing is that Jenny is unharmed and I think her father and Hoa—"

"He made me look like a damn fool! I had him knocked down on the floor and he kicked me . . . I fell down like a clown in the circus. Jenny had to help me up. I was supposed to be protectin' her and her father and . . . hell . . . look at the buzzard now, I showed him!"

A crowd was beginning to collect. From a short distance, Ox's voice boomed, "Let me through!"

Rance Dehner sighed deeply, "Yes, Zeke, you showed him."

Chapter Eighteen

Paul Colten and Scoop Wilsey arrived at the church to find three people and one dog still there. Mandy, Lolly and Tom Bascomb were discussing the events of the evening.

"You two missed an exciting meeting," Mandy spoke playfully to the newcomers. She then spotted the bruises on her husband's face. "What—"

"I ran into a bit of excitement myself," the newspaperman explained. "I'll visit Doctor Cranston tomorrow. He's pretty busy right now." Scoop held up a fist in a bragging manner. "The problems started with a barroom brawl. A lot of gents came away from it with more than just bruises."

Colten gave an account of what had happened in the saloon and at Sammy's Hotel and Restaurant. "Both Jenny and Sammy are fine, so is Hoa."

A quiet moment followed; Mandy ended it as she examined Scoop's face. "Those bruises need attention." She gave Tom a questioning look.

The store owner replied with a smile. "I'll be working late tonight, doing inventory. If you need bandages, salve or anything, just drop by. Bascomb's Emporium is offering free medical supplies to volunteer deputies tonight." He gave a two fingered salute and left.

Scoop fidgeted with his string tie. "So, what all happened at the meeting tonight?"

Mandy pointed a finger down at Clyde who had been wagging his tail in excitement since Scoop entered the church. "This guy almost created a panic when he went running after a black cat who managed to get into the building."

Paul Colten looked troubled. "Why would people panic over a cat?"

Mandy shared the pastor's discomfort. "Tom recognized the animal from my article in today's paper. It was the same black cat Lolly and I saw at the Locke ranch. The cat with an injured eye that Rebecca believed was Satan."

"Tom Bascomb has usually got more sense," Lolly snapped. "Thinkin' it a big deal because the cat that was scarin' Rebecca ends up here in town, what a fool notion!"

"Why was it so foolish?" Colten asked.

Lolly raised her voice in a mockery. "From what I hear the devil enjoys a good fire, that poor feline creature couldn't get away from the smoke and flames at the Locke place fast enough!"

Paul Colten smiled in a mechanical manner. Lolly realized the pastor wanted a serious answer and gave him one. "That poor critter was probably hangin' around the Locke ranch doin' what it could to survive. It ran from the fire and followed Mandy and me back to Grayson. Because of me, we moved pretty slow, wouldn't be hard for the animal to keep up."

Mandy smiled in agreement. "That cat will probably spend what is left of its nine lives here in Grayson. A town with two restaurants is a good place for stray cats."

"I feed scraps to alley cats ever' day," Lolly said. "Like to have 'em 'round, they take care of mice and other small varmints, . . . they're good . . ."

Lolly's voice trailed off as attention shifted to Paul Colten. The pastor seemed to be retreating into himself, only partially aware of the people around him. "A man died tonight, you know," Paul seemed to be talking to himself. "That makes seven people who have been killed in the short time I have been living in Grayson. Yes, some were outlaws but they wouldn't have been here except for me. Jenny Wong came close to being murdered, her father was assaulted and the town almost erupted into a riot. Even a prayer meeting wasn't safe from senseless panic."

Mandy reached out and gently touched the clergyman's arm. "Paul, none of this is your fault."

A curtain of geniality suddenly fell over the pastor, making his companions uneasy. Paul Colten was not a phony and when he tried to put on a phony mask of cheerfulness the result was almost frightening. But there was little the Wilseys and Lolly could do as Colten amicably walked them out of the church. "You're all busy people with things to take care of."

Alone in the sanctuary, Colten sat down on a front pew and tried to pray, not knowing exactly what to pray for. As a young man just graduated from college, his misplaced idealism had led to the death of the woman he loved. He had become a man of violence who gunned down other men for money. Now, as he tried once again to become a man of God, people were getting killed and a town seemed headed for destruction.

His long, tortured prayer ended with a plea for sleep. Since his strange visitor with the lighted torch had appeared, Colten's nights had been restless. Paul lifted himself from the pew and made his way to his office.

Shock charged through the pastor as he opened the office door. At first he denied to himself what he saw. After all, the room was dark with a small window that allowed for only a faint patch of moonlight.

He put a match to the lantern hanging beside the doorway. He could deny what he saw no longer. A noose hung from the ceiling.

Colten remembered a word spoken by the hooded intruder:

"Suicide."

Chapter Nineteen

The sound of a horse neighing caused both Rance Dehner and Ox Bently to pull up their own steeds. "Over there," Dehner pointed to his right where a saddled horse was munching leaves off a tree.

Both men dismounted and approached the animal. The cottonwood's long branches almost blanketed the horse from eyesight on a night when the moon was weak.

"This here must be Butch's horse," Ox said as he patted the sorrel. "Or, if ya want ta git technical it used to be Butch's horse. Wish Zeke hadn't been so fired up 'bout impressin' a female."

Sheriff Bently opened a saddlebag. "Nothin' here but tobacco and a box of ammo, anythin' on your side?"

"Only these," Rance held up a red hood and a very familiar looking toy snake.

Ox gave a mirthless laugh, then once again patted the horse, as if assuring the sorrel that he wasn't going to be blamed for his owner's crimes. "We're dealin' with a group of owlhoots who have a hide-out somewheres out there." He waved a hand at the darkness. "They're keepin' all the loot they've stolen at the hide-out, 'till they finish their job here and then breakup."

"What exactly do you think is their job here?"

"I still think you got it right. They're workin' for someone in Grayson. Someone who hates Reverend Colt, I mean Paul Colten. Meanwhile, I'm keepin' this horse and the saddle at my livery. Accordin' to law, I need to hold on to it for thirty days, and if no one makes a claim, it's mine."

"I'm pretty sure it's yours, Ox."

Butch's sorrel hadn't wandered far. Dehner and Bently were back into town within ten minutes. As they rode to the livery, Rance noticed lights coming from Bascomb's Emporium.

The lights were still on when Dehner was walking to Sammy's Hotel and Restaurant from the livery. Dehner looked inside and caught Tom Bascomb's eye. The store owner motioned for him to come in.

Bascomb was perched on a stool behind a counter, bent over a ledger. "I'm officially closed but I'd be happy to help out if you need anything. Say, did you hear what happened at the church tonight?"

"No."

Tom brought Rance up on the black cat creating a near panic, repeating each detail several times. "I thought a detective from the Lowrie Agency should know all 'bout that."

"Thanks, you've been a big help and, if you don't mind, I could sure use some more information." Dehner placed the red hood on the counter. "What can you tell me about this?"

Tom looked genuinely curious as he examined the item. "This is a fancied up flour bag. Look at the back, you can see part of the brand name coming through the red dye. I sell a whole passel of these things every week, have three sizes: small, medium, and large. This is a small bag." A mischievous look came into Tom's eyes. "Of course, when I sell the bags they still have flour inside!"

Dehner pretended to laugh along with Tom's joke, then asked, "Do people often keep flour bags after the flour's gone?"

"Yeh, lots of folks do, you can put an empty flour bag to good use. I keep some myself."

"Do you sell red dye here?"

"No. There's no demand for it." Tom waved the sack in his hand. "Whoever dyed this thing probably did it somewhere else."

"Why do you say that?"

"In order to get the red dye they would have had to order from me and I would have remembered such an unusual order."

"Couldn't they send for it directly by a catalogue?"

"Sure could," Tom admitted. "But, remember what we talked about a few days ago." He pointed a thumb down the counter where a post office window was set up. "I'm also the postmaster of Grayson. I'm pretty sure I would remember something that came from one of the outfits that make dye."

Dehner placed the toy snake on the counter. Tom took an immediate interest. "That's one of those snakes I read about in the newspaper!"

"Do you sell them?" the detective asked.

"No. I order a lot of do-dads like this at Christmas time. But those snakes are too expensive. A small outfit makes them, that's probably why."

Dehner listened politely to Tom's further accounts of knowing everything that arrived in the mail and thus knowing everything about the town. The detective then thanked Bascomb, stuffed the toy snake and red hood in his back pocket and headed for the hotel.

The night had been cluttered with events for the detective to fit into a pattern. But no pattern emerged as Dehner slowly traipsed down a boardwalk, only confusion.

Stepping into the hotel he saw Jenny standing behind the desk. She smiled and bowed. "I did not have the opportunity to thank you for helping my father and myself earlier this evening."

"No thanks are necessary; how's your father?"

"Doctor Cranston says that a good night's sleep is the best medicine for both my father and Hoa.

They are taking that medicine now." The humor put extra energy into her smile.

Dehner expressed his happiness at both of the Wongs and Hoa being reasonably unscathed by the evening's events and assured Jenny the law would continue to protect them from any trouble Jared Ward might stir up. As he turned toward the stairway he noticed Jenny placing the Back Soon sign on the desk.

The young woman followed behind him toward the stairway. "Mr. Dehner?"

"Yes."

Jenny folded her arms in front of her. "Will you do me the honour of allowing me to accompany you to your room?"

"Wha—"

"My father has allowed me to make this request."

"Wha—"

"You have already done much to help and we are very grateful," Jenny's voice was soft. "But there is yet another favour I must ask of you, a favour which can only be discussed in absolute privacy."

"Well . . . yes . . . sure," Dehner motioned with his arm for the woman to go before him. Jenny paused, as if believing she should not be going first, but then bowed and surrendered to Rance's courtesy.

Dehner quickly glanced around the lobby,

relieved it was empty of people and there was no one to get the wrong idea. As he accompanied Jenny up the stairs, he reflected on all of the strange events of the night.

And the night wasn't finished yet.

Chapter Twenty

As they entered his room, Rance Dehner pointed toward a chair. Jenny spoke before he could issue an invitation to sit down.

"I will remain standing. You are a very busy man. I will take as little of your time as possible."

Dehner noted that the young woman appeared very composed. He hoped he looked the same, despite his nervousness.

"My request is an awkward one, it involves Deputy Zeke Talbot."

"Yes."

"Mr. Dehner, I ask you to speak to Deputy Talbot. He must not try to have . . . a social relationship with me. Of course, he may eat at our restaurant, but perhaps it would be more wise for him to patronize Lolly's Fine Eats."

"Has Zeke done anything to you he shouldn't do?"

"Not in the manner of which you are probably speaking," Jenny said. "But, several times in the past, Zeke has talked with me in an odd manner. He often falls silent and looks at me as if expecting me to declare my affections for him. I have no such affections."

The detective shrugged his shoulders. "A lot of guys become tongue tied around a woman they are trying to impress."

"Tonight Deputy Talbot frightened me."

"How?"

"After the two of you pursued the man called Butch, Deputy Talbot returned to the hotel lobby. He insisted on talking in private with me immediately. I explained that I couldn't, I was busy attending to the needs of my father and Hoa."

"How did Zeke react to that?"

"At first he said nothing but on his face there was tremendous anger. He stayed in the lobby until I took my father and Hoa to their rooms. When I returned Deputy Talbot was still there. He again demanded to see me in private."

The woman stopped speaking. Dehner gently prodded, "And I suspect that you once again refused that request."

Jenny nodded her head and continued. "Deputy Talbot yelled at me. He said he had killed a man for me. His face was twisted, he seemed unable to control himself. The man began to yell things I couldn't understand."

"Was there anyone else in the lobby to witness this?"

"No, but one of our customers yelled, 'Stop all that racket.' The yell came from this floor. Deputy Talbot must have awakened the man. After that, the deputy left, slamming the door behind him."

"Jenny, you should tell your story to Ox Bently."

The woman shook her head. "I know Zeke Talbot is only a step away from becoming the next sheriff of Grayson. Perhaps he will be a good sheriff that is not for me to judge. I do not wish to harm his chances by telling Ox Bently what has happened."

Rance mused to himself that a night of being put through hell had not diminished Jenny Wong's generous and kind nature. "Jenny, the West needs more people like you and your father."

The young woman smiled pleasantly but there was a trace of confusion in it.

"I will talk to Zeke," the detective assured her. "I hope he will get the idea, but if he doesn't, let me know or tell Ox. If he doesn't respect your request then he doesn't have what it takes to be sheriff."

Jenny's smile became stronger. She bowed, thanked Rance for all he had done for her and her father and then left.

Dehner began to pace about the room. He felt exhausted but unable to sit down. He stared out the small window in his room which afforded a view of the street below. Everything appeared calm after a violent night. But Dehner couldn't shake the feeling that, somewhere in Grayson, dangerous things were happening.

Zeke Talbot stepped into the dark room lit only by one candle situated on a table. On the wall hung that strange looking thing, a circle with a star in it, a penta-something. He remembered the first time he had visited this room. He had been overwhelmed by the mystical power that seemed to reside here.

"You lied to me!" he spoke in a low angry whisper. Even now, he could not raise his voice in this place.

"You must be patient," the calm voice of the person sitting at the table seemed to mock him. "I have been patient, and our master has brought me close to what I want. I'm almost there!"

"Well, the master ain't done a damn thing for me!"

"Quiet. You do not speak of Satan in such a manner."

"I'll speak of Satan any way I want," Zeke asserted. "And there ain't nothin' you can do 'bout it."

He was wrong.

Chapter Twenty-One

"Go for your gun, mister, or die!"

Reverend Colt went for his gun. He fired two bullets into the young adversary, who dropped his weapon and stumbled about.

"Please Reverend Colt, don't shoot again," the young man pleaded as blood gushed from his chest. "Turn me over to the law, that's the way things are supposed to work!"

Colt paused only for a moment before he fired a hail of bullets into the young gunman whose body rose into the air, twisted violently, then plunged to the floor. A deafening roar of laughter followed.

Colt looked around at a saloon full of grotesque creatures laughing at him. The saloon was huge and extended forever like a vast desert. Perched on the bar was a gigantic, obese creature with red eyes and claws like an eagle. His teeth resembled spears. Corpses lay on both sides of the monster. The bodies of men Reverend Colt had killed. As the creature laughed, flames shot from his nostrils. Colt realized he was looking directly at the devil.

Beelzebub pointed downward toward a creaking sound. Reverend Colt's eyes also glanced down as a large trap door opened and the fires of Hell blazed upward consuming the saloon and everyone in it.

The preacher opened his eyes. The surrounding darkness brought him relief. There was no fire. A nightmare harms no one.

Shuffling sounds came from the sanctuary. Paul Colten thought he heard a slight creak, perhaps the front door. Could that sound in his dream have been put there by an actual noise?

Paul slowly lifted himself off the cot in his office. After the violence and chaos of the night, he had fallen asleep with his clothes on. The preacher lit a candle that rested on his desk. In sock feet he made his way toward the office door ignoring the lantern hanging beside it. A candle could be easily doused if there was trouble, and Colten sensed trouble.

But, maybe not: earlier in the week, there had been another late night visitor. While he always locked the door to his office, Colten left the front door of the church unlocked. It seemed wrong to do otherwise. A drunk, not wanting to sleep it off outdoors, had stumbled into the church. The same thing could have happened on this night.

Colten opened his office door and stepped out. He held the candle in one hand and a gun in the other. Before handling the .45, he had instinctively flexed his right hand, testing how well he could use it.

The preacher wondered if his instincts would

always be toward weapons and killing. He had abandoned his calling once before and become a gun for hire. Maybe his injured right arm was God's way of keeping him from once again becoming a gunfighter.

Colten silently chastised himself. He was entering a dark sanctuary carrying a lighted candle. That made him an easy target. He needed to concentrate on the moment.

He walked toward the pews. His circle of light only cast the slightest illumination on the back pew but he thought he saw a bulge there, probably another drunk sleeping it off. As he made his way down the center aisle, he could see that the intruder was bleeding.

Paul Colten hurried his footsteps, then stopped and looked down in terror at the man lying in a widening pool of blood. The corpse was that of Zeke Talbot. His throat had been cut.

"You killed him, Preacher, now drop that weapon."

The .45 clattered against the floor as a figure emerged from the dark corner beside the front door. He was wearing a red hood and holding a gun. He stepped into the center aisle of the church, only a couple of yards from Colten.

"Who are you?"

"Let's stick to the matter at hand, Preacher. How many more good people need to be butchered like cattle before you do the right thing?"

"And just what is the right thing?"

The flickering candle cast erratic light on the gunman, making it look like he was on fire. "You already know the answer to that question. You've seen the noose hanging in your office. Use it."

Paul glanced sideways and once again beheld the corpse lying on the church's back pew. For a moment, he wondered if this wasn't a continuation of his nightmare. No, he had to keep a hold on himself. He took a few steps forward. "What kind—"

The hooded figure cocked his gun. "Stop right there! We're tired of you stalling around, Reverend Colt. You have until noon tomorrow. If you're still alive then some terrible things are gonna happen. Many more good people are gonna die and their blood will be on your hands."

"Who's we? Wha—"

"No questions. You know what you gotta do." The hooded man took a few cautious steps backward. "Don't try coming after me, Preacher. You gotta a bad gun hand and I don't. Besides, you could end up with sore feet." He pointed at Colten's socked feet, laughed harshly and left.

Colten didn't try to pursue the gunman. He looked once again at the body of Zeke Talbot. Was there any chance Zeke was still alive? Paul looked at the deputy's arm dangling from the pew over the floor. He felt the wrist and silently chastised himself for even thinking there was a chance Zeke was still living.

A myriad of thoughts pounded through the pastor's head. He needed to get Ox Bently, Rance Dehner, the doctor, the undertaker, he needed to tell the whole world that another bloody death of an innocent had happened because of him.

But he couldn't do any of that. Not now. He needed to escape, if only for a few minutes from the hell that surrounded him.

A drop of candle wax hit his hand causing a slight burn. Paul Colten steadied his hold on the candle as he returned to his office. He placed both the candle and the .45 on his desk. He fidgeted nervously for a moment and then opened the bottom desk drawer.

He slowly pulled out the noose. Why had he kept it? Colten looked at the rope and then at the gun lying on his desk. They both could accomplish the same thing, end this living hell. The end of his life could save others.

He knew such thoughts were insane and yet . . .

Paul Colten dropped to his knees and tried to pray. Instead, he broke out in uncontrolled crying.

Chapter Twenty-Two

Chunks of gray splattered against the black of night as Ox Bently and Rance Dehner walked from the undertaker's establishment to the sheriff's office. Both men were silent.

Ox spoke softly as he unlocked the office. "I didn't feel right leavin' Paul alone but he kept insistin'—"

Dehner interrupted. "Paul Colten is in a very hard fight right now, but there's nothing you or I can do to help him."

Once they were inside the office with the door closed, Ox angrily slammed his fist on the desk. "Zeke must have found out who's behind all this devil stuff. Instead of comin' ta us, he decided to be a big hero, probably wanted to impress Jenny . . ." Ox's voice began to break, "Damn!"

The sheriff walked to the window and looked outside. Nothing there helped. "Guess I didn't do such a good job of trainin' him." He inhaled deeply and then let out his breath. "Like some coffee?"

"Yes, thank you."

As Ox began to fuss with the coffee pot, Dehner spoke in a low voice. "I don't think Zeke found out who is behind all of these killings. I think Zeke was in on it."

Anger flared in the sheriff's eyes. "What the—"

"Just give me a chance to explain."

"Start explainin'."

"We know the people responsible for the murders are using toy snakes and red dye," Dehner said. "Those items aren't sold here in Grayson and, according to the postmaster no one has them sent here by mail."

"So?"

"Zeke Talbot rode shotgun on the stagecoach," Dehner continued. "There are several places he could have bought those items. Hiding those things from Cactus Olsen wouldn't have been tough, he could sneak the toys and the dye into Grayson easily."

Bently's eyes clamped down on his coffee making routine. "That don't mean a thing."

Dehner began to pace slowly around the office. "We are dealing with a true believer, someone who is a Satanist and is obsessed with using the power of the devil to destroy Paul Colten."

The sheriff cut in quickly. "That sure don't describe Zeke none."

"Yes," Dehner agreed. "But, as I see it, our Satanist used up all money on hand to hire Kid Madero and his gang. After that failed, more money was needed."

"Poor Zeke didn't have no money."

A new intensity came into Rance's voice. "But

Zeke knew all about the stagecoach schedule. He could tip off the Satanist when the stagecoach was transporting one thousand dollars in cash."

A look of satisfaction curtained Ox's face. He thought he had found a weakness in Dehner's logic. "And after the owlhoots robbed the stage, they'd ride off with the loot. They wouldn't hang around to do the biddin' of some crazy devil worshiper."

"They would if they had been promised even more money."

"And where'd that come from?"

"The Locke ranch," Dehner answered. "Remember, we found the office desk smashed open where the Lockes probably hid their money."

"What ya say still don't make no sense." The changing tone of Ox's voice indicated Dehner's words were making increasing sense to him. "Zeke don't hold no grudge against Paul Colten. I coulda seen it if he did."

"The Satanist behind this scheme also made a true believer out of Zeke. Remember what Paul told us, people become devil worshipers because they want power. Zeke came to believe that if he served the devil, Satan would give him exactly what he wanted . . . Jenny Wong."

The sheriff poured two cups of coffee. He said nothing as he handed one to Rance.

The detective spoke softly. "Last night, Jenny

told me that Zeke has been acting very strange lately. He'd just sit or stand around and wait for her to declare her love for him."

Ox blew on his coffee and whispered, "Sounds like Zeke was waitin' for Beelzebub to do the heavy liftin' for him."

"I'm afraid so." Dehner continued. "I think the gang of killers who replaced the Madero bunch were instructed to make Zeke look good to Jenny."

Ox's eyes stayed fixed on his coffee cup. "How do ya figger?"

"When the stagecoach was held up, the thugs pretended they had taken Zeke prisoner. One of the gang threatened to abduct Jenny but Zeke declared they would only do so over his dead body and a gang of cold blooded killers gave in immediately. It was all an act!"

Ox began to join Dehner in walking about the office, occasionally sipping coffee. "But last night when Butch attacked Sammy and Jenny, that sure enough weren't no show. Butch ended up dead!"

Dehner nodded. "Butch's death stopped my notions cold. I have been giving it a lot of thought."

Ox gave a slight laugh, "What did ya come up with after all your heavy thinkin'."

"Jared Ward played right into the Satanist's hand. His grief drove him to stir up hate against

Sammy and Jenny. Butch, one of the hired thugs, was tasked with stoking that spark into a raging fire. The idea was to make Paul Colten feel guilty about hurting others, killing Sammy and Jenny was never part of the scheme."

"But—"

Dehner held up a palm and continued. "Butch was supposed to get to Sammy's Hotel and Restaurant, injure Sammy just enough to make things look real and pretend to attempt to kidnap Jenny. Of course, Zeke would stop him. But the deputy got carried away. To use a theatrical term he went off script. He hit Butch hard and called him a coward while he lay on the floor. Butch got mad and struck back. The thug really would have kidnapped Jenny but he burned his arm on the stove."

Ox slammed his now empty coffee cup on to the desk. "It was a bullet from Zeke's gun that killed Butch."

"Zeke couldn't allow Butch to live. The outlaw was mad at him. Who knows what Butch would have spilled if we had arrested him."

The sheriff shook his head. "All these killin's and we still don't know who's behind it."

"No. But our Satanist has got to be getting more and more desperate. Something very big is going to happen soon."

Chapter Twenty-Three

Riley Browder swallowed his last piece of bacon and looked at the two men sitting around the morning campfire with him. "Tobe, Mort, this has been the craziest job I ever had. But, it sure pays good. Don't let yourselfs get used to it. You'll be eating beans a lot more than bacon."

Tobe and Mort exchanged amused glances. Tobe spoke first. "What I'm thinkin' 'bout right now is Mexican food."

Mort exploded in laughter as if his friend had just told a hilarious joke. "Yep, after today, Tobe and me is ridin' south. We're gonna enjoy a lot of spicy food and spicy women."

This time, both men indulged in a long bout of laughter. Riley forced a smile onto his craggy face and thought about how he missed Butch. Butch had been close to his thirty-eight years. Now, he had only these two young fools to finish the job with.

Both Tobe and Mort were somewhere around twenty. Both were ugly as sin but didn't seem to know it. And, Riley mused, both would probably be shot dead soon in some fight over nothing. That's the way their types usually ended up.

Riley Browder was sick of having to work with young thugs. After today, he was starting a new life.

"You headin' for Mexico, Boss?"

Riley had been staring at the fire. He wasn't sure which one of his henchmen had asked the question. "No, I'm riding in the opposite direction. I'm gonna settle down in Montana."

"Montana!" Mort spit the word out. "They say the winters there are somethin' awful."

"They're right. That's why I'm going up there."

"Huh?" Tobe made the guttural sound.

"Montana is wide open," Riley's voice was wistful. "Not too many people, if you steer clear of Bannack and Virginia City where fools are still looking for gold. Many of the towns don't even have law. Good place for a man to get lost."

Mort gave a contemptible guffaw. "Get lost in a snow storm."

Riley Browder continued as if Mort hadn't spoken. "There's plenty of land in Montana. With the money we've made off this job, I'll be able to buy as much land as I want and start a ranch."

"What kind of ranch?"

Tobe's question made Browder realize he really had no definite ideas on the subject. Owning land had always been one of those mystical, unobtainable goals that filled his thoughts, sort of like having a beautiful, faithful wife.

"We've done enough jawing," Riley snapped. "Time to get to work, ain't none of us going anywhere just yet. We got one more killing in front of us."

The three men stood up and began to douse the fire. Mort's face twisted a bit as he looked across the fire at his boss. "What do you think 'bout all this devil stuff? It kinda spooks me."

"I don't think about it. We do our job, collect the money and vamoose."

Riley was lying. He had never worked for a Satanist before and listening to all this palaver about torturing and killing a preacher left him unnerved. Only the thought of more money prodded him on.

He whispered to himself. "One more killing and my life will change."

Chapter Twenty-Four

"We'll probably be Lolly's first customers ag'in," Ox said to Rance as they approached Lolly's Fine Eats. He was wrong. Doctor Fred Cranston sat in the restaurant drinking coffee and talking with the establishment's owner, who stood beside his table. They both looked grim and it occurred to Dehner that this was the first time he had seen Lolly and the doctor when they weren't engaged in some mock argument.

Of course, the grimness was appropriate. Ox and Rance sat at the same table as the doctor. Lolly took their breakfast orders then brought the sheriff and the detective cups of coffee much better than what they had just consumed at the sheriff's office.

"I was just telling Lolly," Doc Cranston nodded at Lolly, who remained standing. "I'm worried plenty about Paul Colten. Finding Zeke's body, and then hearing what that gunman told him about killing himself before noon today. I think someone should stay with Paul at least for the next twenty-four hours."

"Paul won't let anyone stay with him, Doc," frustration laced Ox's voice. "Sure, he'll tell us ever' detail, feels obligated to be truthful. But it ends there."

155

"From what he did tell us, I suspect the gang leader doesn't have too much confidence in his henchmen."

Ox seemed to ponder Rance's statement. "How do ya figger?"

"Paul told us he didn't spot any blood on the gunman's body," Dehner answered. "If one man had carried Zeke's body inside the church, there would be blood all over him. The gunman had help carrying the body but ordered his buddies out. Probably afraid they would do something stupid when he was pushing the pastor to kill himself."

"You're right," the doctor commented, "but that doesn't help Paul any. Maybe I should try dropping by, I could come up with an excuse."

"As soon as the breakfast crowd leaves, I'm gonna see Paul Colten," Lolly declared. "And I don't need no fool excuse!"

The sheriff looked puzzled. "What d'ya mean?"

"Reverend Paul Colten has hisself an appointment this afternoon to meet Jared Ward at his ranch. I helped make that appointment and I intend to remind Reverend Colten he's the pastor of this town's one church and he's got a job to do."

The sheriff still looked puzzled. "How did ya get involved with makin' this appointment, Lolly?"

"Last night, after all the hullabaloo, Jared came

by to see me. I did feel sorry for him. Anyone would be he looked so lost. The seriousness of what he done had sobered him up some. He tole me he didn't feel worthy of stepping inside a church again. As for Jenny and Sammy, he couldn't face them. But he wanted to talk to the Reverend. Afternoons would be best, 'cause that's when the work at the ranch slows down some. I tole him I'd set it up for Paul to visit him this afternoon and I did."

Doc Cranston smiled approval. "You did a fine thing. Helping other people is the best way Paul Colten can help himself."

A group of six people sauntered into the restaurant and sat down. Lolly beamed a smile in their direction. "Things are picking up. I'd better stop jawin' and start workin'. Your food will be out in a minute."

Ox watched appreciatively as the woman hurried to serve the new arrivals. "Lolly sure works hard."

"And it's paid off," the doc added. "This restaurant has always done well."

"Lolly's a fine woman," Ox said, "but I don't agree with her on ever'thing."

Dehner looked a bit surprised. "I don't follow you."

"Lolly has sympathy for Jared Ward but I don't, not no more," Ox replied. "Jared's been through some rough times, I ain't sayin' different. I can

157

unnerstand his actin' a bit strange. But stirrin' up a mob against Sammy and his daughter, I just can't—"

"You've never been married, have you, Ox?"

The sheriff was obviously stunned by Doc Cranston's question. "Ah, no."

The conversation halted as plates of food were set in front of the three men. After they had all taken a bite or two of their food the doctor began to speak again. "I was married for three years. My wife died before either one of us made it to thirty. I still remember that first horrible year of living without her."

"Doc, I'm sorry . . ."

Ox was obviously surprised to learn about Fred Cranston's past despite the fact they had lived in the same town for many years. Dehner figured the doctor was a very private man and, for some reason, Paul Colten's dilemma had touched something inside him and caused him to open up.

"That all happened a long time ago, Ox," the doctor continued. "But I can understand how Jared went off the rails."

The doctor pushed his food around on the plate, then decided to continue. "She asked one thing of me before she died . . . to do everything I could to give our son a good life. Carl was two when Sharon died."

Ox's voice was reduced to a whisper. "You have a son?"

The doctor's eyes stayed down. "Not anymore. I wasn't much of a father. Carl became wild, I couldn't control him, gave up after a while. He came to a bad end."

Dehner realized Ox was too shocked to say anything. "Don't blame yourself, Doctor Cranston. I'm sure you did the best you could."

Doc Cranston gave Rance a wistful smile. "I'm afraid that advice comes a bit late." He took a long sip of coffee, then smiled again in a more robust manner. "You gents have more important things to do than listen to an old man's regrets. For that matter, so does this old man. Let's enjoy our breakfast, then get to work!"

The sudden change in Fred Cranston reminded Dehner of the time he had attended a play rehearsal in Dallas. He had an intense talk with an actor who was receiving death threats. After the conversation, the actor jumped on stage and became the magnificently hilarious Falstaff. How much of Doc Cranston's life was given over to being an actor playing a role?

Dehner's musings continued as the three men finished breakfast and followed the doctor's prescription to, "get to work." *What was it Shakespeare wrote in* As You Like It, *"All the world's a stage and . . ."*

The detective ridded his mind of such philosophical speculation. With Zeke Talbot dead, he had plenty of tasks to do as a volunteer deputy and, of course, there was the matter of killers to be stopped and a Satanist to be uncovered.

After leaving Lolly's Fine Eats, Rance headed for the *Grayson Herald*. He had promised Paul Colten to give Scoop and Mandy Wilsey all of the available information regarding the murder of Zeke Talbot. The only catch: the pastor didn't want the newspaper people to visit him.

"But why?" Mandy's voice was almost a plea.

"All he would say is that he's not ready to talk with anyone yet."

The journalists felt a bit better when Dehner told them of Colten's appointment with Jared Ward but only a little bit. Still, they got busy composing the details of Zeke Talbot's murder. In a couple of hours, they would post the story beside the door of the newspaper office. That was a place the townspeople often visited on days when the newspaper didn't publish.

Paul Colten sat in his office trying to focus on the sermon he was preparing for Sunday. His mind kept returning to all of the funerals he had performed lately. How many more would he have—

A loud thud jerked him from his thoughts. The sound might have been a rock slamming against the side of the church. Paul bolted from his chair and looked outside the office window. He saw nothing, but the window was small, not allowing him much of a view.

The pastor returned to his desk and once again attempted to force his mind onto the sermon. He had almost succeeded when a low groaning sound came from the sanctuary. Paul Colten remembered the words Lolly Farnum had been told by the people who butchered Sarah Locke, "Satan doesn't need darkness. He strikes in sunshine too."

Colten mumbled a private reprimand. He couldn't allow himself to be cowed by vicious killers. He had dealt with their kind before.

Another groan sounded from the sanctuary, this one louder. Paul began to open a bottom drawer where he kept his gun. Pressing his lips together in anger with himself, he slammed the drawer shut and stormed out of the office unarmed. He needed to start handling problems without a gun.

Stepping into the sanctuary, the pastor spotted nothing unusual but he could hear the sound of arms and legs awkwardly shuffling about.

Colten shouted angrily, "Whoever you are, show yourself!"

A ghostly figure covered in white sprang up from one of the middle pews. It moved into the center aisle and began to walk toward Colten. "I'm a spirit of the devil, here ta warn ya."

Paul looked carefully at the grotesque apparition moving toward him. It was a man covered in flour . . . Pecos!

The front doors of the church opened, Rance Dehner hurried inside and down the aisle. He grabbed Pecos by the arm and spoke to the pastor. "I just came from Bascomb's Emporium. Tom told me this character had just been in and stolen a small sack of flour."

Colten looked confused. "Why would he do that?"

"Tom made the mistake in the past of giving Pecos money," Dehner answered. "Now when Tom refuses to hand over cash, Pecos grabs something and runs."

"I ain't never stole no flour before," Pecos declared.

"True," Dehner conceded. "Most of the time you grab candy but today Tom was standing near the candy jars."

The detective looked at Colten. "I noticed a small trail of flour starting in an alley beside the store and followed it here."

Pecos's voice became a plea. "I figgered you'd enjoy a little joke, Preacher. Maybe show yore thanks with some money, not much mind ya but . . ."

Colten shook his head. "Pecos, this is not the way to seek Christian charity."

Paul Colten watched as Dehner escorted his prisoner out the double doors. Pecos was hardly representative of a citizen of Grayson. Still, how many people in the town were going off the rails because of all this devil talk going around?

As the clergyman returned to his office, it occurred to him that what had just happened was funny. Still, he found it impossible to even smile.

After seeing that Pecos was bedded down for a long nap in one of Grayson's three jail cells, Dehner headed for Sammy's Hotel and Restaurant. He hoped Jenny might provide him with information which could lead to finding out who had conned Zeke into believing the devil would help him with his love life. It was a long shot but worth a try.

But Rance had lost touch with the time. It was now past noon and Jenny was busy serving lunch. Dehner returned to the sheriff's office, allowing Ox to take a break.

When the sheriff returned, the lunch hour was almost over and Dehner made his way back to the hotel-restaurant. The proprietor, as usual, was bustling about behind the registration desk.

"Welcome," Sammy said quickly then moved to the point. "I have read posting at newspaper office about Zeke Talbot. Very unfortunate. I'm sure you will catch the murderer soon."

"Thanks," Dehner replied. "How can you be so sure?"

"According to story, person behind all these

murders is a Satanist. All Satanists are on the wrong side. Get caught."

Dehner wasn't sure if Sammy was being serious, joking or, in all likelihood, a bit of both. He settled for nodding his head and not saying anything as a black cat jumped up on the registration desk.

"Hello, Wild Bill," Sammy said affectionately as he petted the cat.

Dehner took a look at the feline's face containing a scar and a partially closed eye. "Is Wild Bill your cat?"

"No one ever own a cat. Sammy not sure who first said those wise words. But very sure it was not Confucius."

"But does Wild Bill hang out here much?"

"Sometimes yes, sometimes no, we feed Wild Bill because he chase mice. Sometimes he catch and kill them. Good guy to have around. But sometimes disappear for a while. According to *Grayson Herald*, Wild Bill also out at Locke ranch. Maybe Mrs. Locke feed him and he catch mice there too."

"The Locke ranch is a long way for the cat to wander off . . ."

Dehner fell silent for several minutes. When he spoke again, it sounded almost like he was talking to himself. "You know, Sammy, I came here to ask your daughter questions on the slight hope she might be able to give me some idea who

164

was behind all the killings. I think Wild Bill just gave me all the clues I need."

The proprietor smiled and held up an index finger. "I tell daughter Wild Bill know more than she. Pretty girl need to be made humble now and again. Very wise saying by Sammy . . ."

"And not Confucius!" Rance Dehner quickly left Sammy and stood on the boardwalk outside of the hotel. He stared at nothing while ideas began to form a pattern in his mind. "I've been a fool!" he suddenly declared in a sharp whisper.

The detective hopped off the boardwalk and began a fast run down the main street to the church. He stopped half way spotting Mandy Wilsey who was coming from the direction of the church.

"Have you seen Clyde?" The woman tried to make the question sound casual but her eyes were moist.

"No, afraid not, have you just been to see Paul Colten?"

"I tried to. I thought maybe Clyde had wandered up to the church. But Paul isn't there, guess he's heading out to the Ward place." Mandy looked around frantically then called out her dog's name. There was no response. "Clyde always stays close to Scoop and me. He rarely goes outside for very long . . ."

"Do you know when Paul left?"

"No."

Once again, matters began to clarify in the detective's mind. A lot of seemingly unconnected events began to tie together. "Sorry, Mandy, but . . . see you later." Rance turned and began to run back in the direction of the sheriff's office.

"Where are you going?" The newspaperwoman shouted to Dehner's back.

"To find your dog!"

Chapter Twenty-Five

Paul Colten rode toward the Ward ranch trying to quell the fear inside him. He was afraid he'd find Jared Ward dead, his body mutilated. The pastor tried to tell himself the notion was absurd, but was it? He had witnessed the horrible killing of Sally Ward by Kid Madero and only a few hours ago Zeke Talbot's body was lying on a pew in the church, blood dripping to the floor.

Cactus Olsen had been gunned down and Rebecca Locke mercilessly stabbed to death. All of these fine people would still be alive if he had not come to town. At first Colten had been determined to find out who was behind these murders, figuring it almost had to be revenge killings by someone for one of the five men he had killed as Reverend Colt.

Paul allowed his horse to detour toward a small creek near the road. The day was hot and the horse needed refreshment. He remained in the saddle as his cayuse drank. Somehow, finding the Satanist behind all these horrors no longer seemed very important to him. He'd leave that task to Ox Bently and Rance Dehner.

The horse stopped drinking and Paul gently turned him back onto the road. The important thing for him was to do whatever it took to stop the horror. Whatever it took . . .

Colten tried to get control over his emotions. He sighed deeply and felt the hot sun on his back. He really didn't need the frock coat he was wearing. A crooked grin crossed his face as he mused that two categories of professionals have a proclivity to wear a frock coat: gamblers and preachers.

"Maybe we have more in common than I would have thought," Colten said aloud.

The pastor spotted someone riding toward him—riding very slow. Not too unusual, after all, the day was hot. Colten wondered if whoever it was knew about the creek. Maybe he should mention it but, of course, it was easy to spot and the horse would instinctively—

As the rider drew closer, Colten could see he was hunched over, perhaps unconscious. Terror once again gripped Paul Colten. Could this be Jared Ward tied to his saddle, dead?

"Get ahold of yourself!" Colten again spoke aloud. "Someone may be in trouble."

Paul kneed his horse into a fast canter, and pulled up beside the hunched figure. "Hello there," he shouted, "are you all right?!"

The figure quickly unfolded, sitting erect in the saddle with a Remington .44 pointed at Colten. "Why, I'm jus' fine, thank you kindly, Preacher."

Paul looked quizzically at the gunman. "I think I recognize your voice. I heard it not very long ago."

"That's right, Preacher," Riley Browder proclaimed heartily. "You and me exchanged a few words this morning. I tole you to end your life before noon. But you wouldn't listen, so now I gotta do the job for you." He waved his gun, motioning for Colten to keep riding. "I'll be right behind you giving orders. One bad move and you're dead."

They didn't stay on the main road long. Browder ordered Colten onto a side trail which led to a dry arroyo. They rode in the arroyo for a while and then came out into an area with a forked trail. "Left, Preacher."

Less than five minutes later, Browder exclaimed in mock joy, "Hallelujah, Preacher, we've reached the place where you'll enter the pearly gates."

Paul Colten noted Kid Madero had made a similar claim about the pearly gates. He hoped the results would be similar, but doubted it.

Colten also surmised that the area looked very pleasant and under different circumstances he would have enjoyed it. They were at the bottom of a large hill. Thick trees covered the bottom half of the hill, then stopped and gave way to dirt, stones and a collection of large boulders at the very top.

The remains of a campfire were evident. Horses were tied up at nearby trees. The surrounding grass was green with only a light touch of brown. Despite the dry arroyo, there was water nearby.

But the scene was far from delightful. Two hardcases were waiting at the camp, tobacco stained drool came from both of their mouths. One of the larger trees had a noose dangling from it.

Colten kept his voice buoyant, matching that of his captor. "Looks to me like you fellas have been camped out here for a spell. You picked a great spot."

"Yeh, but we're getting tired of it. Want to move on." Browder's voice turned harsh. "Get off your horse, Preacher."

The preacher complied. Browder dismounted, both men ground tethered their horses, and then Browder pushed his captive toward the two henchmen. "My name's Riley. These here gents are Mort and Tobe. Tobe is the one wearing the old derby. That hat sure is ugly but don't worry none, you won't have to look at it for long."

Both Tobe and Mort laughed loudly. "Keep an eye on the pulpit pounder," their boss ordered as he holstered his gun, turned to his horse and began to undo a saddlebag.

Both of Browder's hands were full as he walked toward his captive: a book in one hand and a bottle of ink and a pen in the other. He held up the tome, and mockingly proclaimed, "*Frontier*

Truths by Reverend Paul Colten, recognize the couple on the cover, Reverend Colt?"

Paul Colten was stunned. He had destroyed his own copy of *Frontier Truths* after his wife's murder. The Wilseys owned a copy, but knowing the cover would bring him pain, had never shown it to the pastor. That cover featured a drawing of Paul and his wife standing in front of their church in Sterling, Arizona. Both of them had confident smiles; they were looking forward to a happy, purposeful life together.

Colten took his eyes off the book. He needed to keep his mind clear, not have it flooded with painful memories.

Riley Browder maintained the mockery in his voice. "Now I hear tell when you meet up with a famous writer, you should ask him to sign a copy of his book, why, it might could become a keepsake."

Colten quickly assessed his situation. Riley Browder stood directly beside him. Mort and Tobe were standing together a few feet in front, guns drawn. If there was any way out, Paul couldn't spot it.

"Now, I'm gonna ask you to sign the book in a special way. You're to write," Browder paused, his eyebrows lifted as if igniting his memory. "Ever'thing I've preached is lies. I'm going to meet my master, Satan."

Colten maintained the mock cordiality. "Let

171

me guess, you're going to hang me and then leave the book right under my dangling body. When I'm eventually found, people will think I gave my life to Satan and then committed suicide."

Riley shrugged his shoulders. "Yeh, but it's a bit more complicated than that. We're gonna take this book to a certain someone who is gonna pay us good. Then we ride back and drop the book near your carcass which the vultures will already be feasting on."

"I'm not doing it."

The firmness in Colten's voice ended the charade of genteel politeness. "Do what I say or we'll kill you," Browder mumbled.

"You're going to kill me anyway."

"Yep, but maybe we got a way of changing your mind 'bout writing in the book." Browder looked in the direction of his henchmen. "Tobe, did you carry out the little task I gave you?"

"Shore did, boss."

"Show the pulpit pounder what you picked up in Grayson."

Tobe grinned, holstered his gun, and did a fast walk into the trees. Colten closed his eyes in anguish as he heard a familiar barking sound laced with Tobe's curses. The gunny returned carrying Clyde in his arms.

"I'm getting impatient, Preacher," Browder spit the words out. "You do what I say, or we don't jus' kill the dog, we cut him up and throw the pieces in front of the newspaper office."

Tobe was holding Clyde, who struggled in his arms. Riley Browder had a book and pen in his hands. Only Mort's gun was still pointing at their captive. Paul Colten realized this was as good as it was going to get.

The pastor began to swing his right arm as he spoke to Browder. "I'll bet you and your pals were in the Mule Kick on the night Butch prodded Jared Ward."

"Yeh, so?"

"Then you saw me gun down that fool kid."

Browder's face crunched into an angry glare. "What are you getting at?"

"I'm wearing a Derringer on my wrist," Colten lied. "The gun has two bullets. Turn the dog loose, Browder, or I'll fire both bullets into you."

"Mort will kill you!"

"I'm going to die no matter what, this way I have the satisfaction of taking you with me."

Paul Colten swung his right arm up, Browder dropped everything in his hands and lurched backwards. Colten delivered a hard kick to Browder's knee and the killer went down. Colten hit the ground as a bullet from Mort's gun whined over him.

Tobe tossed Clyde aside and drew his gun as Browder scrambled onto his feet. Colten also buoyed up, slammed a left fist into the boss man's face and moved behind him as he stumbled. Colten now had Browder between him and the other two killers.

With Clyde attacking his heels, Tobe moved sideways and fired. His bullet cut into Riley Browder's midsection.

The head outlaw yelled in pain, before shouting, "Damn you idiots, hold fire!"

Paul Colten wrapped his left arm around Browder's neck and pressed his right fist against the boss man's back. "Stay away, both of you, or your boss man is dead."

Tobe anxiously shouted to Mort. "Don't shoot! Browder's the only one who knows who the Satan jasper is . . . we need him to get the rest of our money."

"Yeh," Mort snickered. "Besides, the preacher man ain't got that good a hand. We can stop him."

Mort was right and the preacher man knew it. Despite the bullet wound to his abdomen, Browder was managing a hard struggle, making it impossible for Colten to take his gun. Paul dragged the killer a few feet up the hill to the trees and then dropped him. Browder again yelled in pain but still managed to turn around and see his adversary's hands.

Another shot winged over the preacher's head. Colten ran into a dense thicket of trees. He then moved cautiously not wanting to announce his location. He could hear the two henchmen talking with Riley Browder.

"You OK, boss?"

"Yes, get after the pulpit pounder!"

"We gotta be careful, he's got a Derringer."

"You damn fools, that was a trick, he's unarmed, get the hell after him."

Both Tobe and Mort gave out with loud yelps. They were about to have some fun.

Colten maneuvered through the trees. He had little time to come up with a plan but figured playing hide and seek with two armed thugs would not turn out well. He moved out of the thicket and began to advance stealthily up the hill. His steps were fast but quiet. Maybe he could make it over the hill without being spotted.

"There he goes, Tobe!"

So much for plan A, Colten broke into a fast run toward the hill's crest. Two shots whistled in his direction but both gunmen were also running, marring their accuracy.

Exuberance shot through Colten's entire body. Despite the circumstances, he was almost enjoying himself. For some time he had been focused on his weaknesses, spiritual and physical. Yes, one arm might be injured but both of his legs were strong. Joyous laughter flowed from the preacher as he put more and more distance between himself and his pursuers.

Reaching the hill's top, he leaned against

a large boulder and chuckled happily. But it quickly occurred to him that he had little to laugh or be happy about. He peeked around the boulder. Tobe and Mort weren't far away.

Both killers knew he didn't have a gun. They probably assumed he was running down the other side of the hill. Why not surprise them?

The idea was crazy but Paul Colten was not a man with a lot of options. The pastor took a step back and then, putting as much of the burden on his legs as he could he began to push against the boulder. The large stone began to move but only slightly. Colten was pushing with his left shoulder but a hot flame still ignited in his injured right shoulder. The pain almost made Colten surrender.

The preacher whispered to himself in a voice twisted with pain: *"No man having put his hand to the plough, and looking back, is fit for the kingdom of God."* He couldn't say anything else. Nausea made speaking impossible. Colten felt faint but he kept pushing.

The huge stone came loose and plummeted down the hillside. Paul Colten plummeted behind it. He tried to stop his fall but couldn't. He felt like one of the smaller pebbles following the boulder in an avalanche-like descent.

A loud cry cut through the pounding sound of the boulder. The huge rock stopped and Colten's body splayed against it. He got up, looking for enemies in the swirling dust cloud. He stumbled about and then watched the ground rise up and swallow him.

Tobe crawled over to his gun and grabbed it before returning to his feet. He had jumped out of the way of the oncoming rock slide in time. He didn't know about Mort or the preacher man and he'd have to wait until the massive dust cloud settled before he could find out.

The gunman spotted shadowy movement in the descending cloud but couldn't identify it. Harsh particles from the cloud swept into his eyes blurring his vision. After he had blinked them out the figure had vanished. Cries of pain came from Mort who lay on the ground beside the boulder.

Placing one hand near his eyes as a shield and holding his gun in the other, Tobe kneeled beside the squirming Mort. "How you doin', pard?"

"Leg . . . hurt bad."

"Seen the preacher man?"

"Na . . . thought I heard him walkin' 'round though."

Tobe nodded, returned to his feet and crept around to the other side of the large rock where Paul Colten lay unconscious. "Well . . . looks like the good Reverend is in a perty bad way."

A sense of giddiness overwhelmed Tobe. The

preacher man was in no condition to resist any longer. Riley Browder lay wounded and would be entirely dependent on him to help finish up the job. Mort couldn't do nothin'.

Tobe realized he was now the most powerful man in this operation. The only one who could stand on his own two feet. If only he knew who the crazy Satan guy was but he didn't. He needed Browder but Mort . . .

An ugly grin covered Tobe's face as he returned to the other side of the boulder. Mort looked up at him quizzically. "Find the preacher?"

"Yeh, passed out, he's in real bad shape, won't give us any more trouble."

"Good," Mort's voice took on a pleading quality. "I think my leg's broke. You're gonna have to help me, maybe take some tree branches and make up—"

Tobe shrugged his shoulders. "I'm 'fraid I ain't got no time for doctorin'. Hell, the boss man's bleedin' bad. One cripple is 'bout all I have time to deal with. Besides, a two-way split means more money than a three-way split. Simple arithmetic.

Mort's already pale face turned the colour of water as it contorted in shock and terror. "Tobe, we're pards," he could think of little else to say and babbled, "you know what people say 'bout pards . . ."

"Sure do, but you know what else people say."

Mort's lips were trembling, "Wha—"

"There's no honour among thieves," Tobe laughed as he pulled the trigger.

"Looks like they changed course here," Rance Dehner said. Ox Bently nodded his head in agreement and both men guided their horses out of the arroyo. They quickly arrived at the area where the forked trail began.

"Damn!" Bently shouted.

"I'll see what I can find," Dehner dismounted and began to study the ground.

A shot sounded. Dehner got back on his horse and both men began a quick gallop.

"What the hell is goin' on?"

"The preacher is unconscious!" Tobe yelled back to his boss.

"Leave him for a moment and get back here quick, both of you."

Tobe followed orders and ran to where his boss lay. Browder had taken off his bandana and pressed it against his wound.

"Where's Mort?"

"He's dead."

Riley Browder asked no questions about Mort's death, which didn't surprise Tobe. Browder was that kind of boss and they were in that kind of business.

Browder looked in the direction of the trail.

"I've heard hoofbeats, can't hear them now but someone's coming."

"Maybe the Satan guy, with—"

"No," Browder declared firmly. "It's trouble." He pointed to his horse nibbling grass nearby. "Grab the Winchester from my saddle and hide out in the woods. From there you can keep an eye on the preacher if he comes to. What's comin' is law or people who can spill to the law. I'm losin' blood and my .44 won't be much help against the odds. But they won't see you. I don't know how many's comin' but you should be able to pick 'em off, what with the rifle and your pistol."

"Right, Boss!"

Riley Browder watched his henchman run to the chestnut, retrieve the rifle and head into the woods. Tobe was a fool, but Browder had spent most of his life with fools and thought Tobe could handle the job.

"I hope, this time, the idiot doesn't shoot me," the outlaw said under his breath. He was sure Tobe had killed Mort to get a bigger cut of the money. But Riley knew he was safe because Tobe didn't know the name of the Satanist. That was a smart move on his part, the mark of a man who would get what he wanted.

Browder spotted two specks on the trail, rapidly growing bigger. There were only two of them! Yes, this part of the job should be easy enough.

· · ·

Rance Dehner returned the field glasses to his saddlebag. "I could only spot one man. He's lying on the ground and may be hurt. There's two horses nearby, one of them could be Paul's cayuse. May be more horses tied up somewhere. That's all I can tell you."

"Still mad at myself," Ox muttered. "An old law dog like me shoulda knowed better than to spur our nags into a fast run. We might as well sent a telegram sayin' we was comin'."

Rance grimaced and nodded his head. "I followed right behind you."

The old law dog continued. "The way I see it, our best bet now is jus' to ride in careful like but put on we're good Samaritans. We heard a shot and wanted to make sure nobody got hurt. Of course, we might change all that real quick. This ain't exactly a situation where you can map out a plan."

Tobe watched as two horsemen rode into the camp. They dismounted in the same area where Browder and the preacher had ground tethered their steeds. He thought both men took long glances at the preacher's cayuse.

They began to walk toward the boss man. The closer they got the better targets they made.

Moaning sounds cut the air. Tobe turned and focused on the area around the boulder. The preacher man was on his feet and leaning against the rock.

Tobe cursed himself inwardly. Soon, the preacher would find Mort's body. "I didn't take Mort's gun," the killer whispered. "The preacher man might have it soon."

Tobe lifted the Winchester to take down the pulpit pounder, but stopped. The preacher man still had to write in that book. He couldn't kill him yet.

A confused Tobe returned his eyes to the scene with his boss and the newcomers. Things had changed some. He would have to wait.

Rance and the sheriff dismounted a fair distance from the wounded outlaw. They ground tethered their horses and approached the camp with caution. "I'll keep an eye on the wounded fella," Ox said in a low voice. "Ya keep lookin' at those trees, might be somethin' interestin' goin' on there."

Dehner mumbled assent. As the two men drew near to Browder, a loud yapping sound came from the trees, followed by scampering steps.

"Clyde!" Ox exclaimed as he bent down and picked up the animal. Clyde began to cover his friend's face with appreciative licks.

Dehner had already told the sheriff Clyde was missing and passed along his theory that the animal had been kidnapped as a tool to manipulate Paul Colten. Ox kept the dog in his arms as he and Dehner walked over to Browder and crouched beside him.

Ox skipped the cordial greetings as he removed the pistol from Riley Browder's holster. "I see you're shot, we'll get to all that. But don't waste time blabberin' some stupid story. I recognize the cayuse and I sure recognize this dog."

The excitement of being with friends overwhelmed Clyde. He could stay in Ox's arms no longer. He jumped loose and crossed to the other side of the wounded killer where Rance Dehner was crouched. Dehner petted the dog while following instructions and watching for anything unusual in the trees.

Bently pointed a threatening finger at Riley Browder, "You're gonna tell me where Paul Colten is and you're gonna do it right now."

"Sure, look I ain't stupid, I'll go along with anything you want," Browder's surrender sounded too melodramatic. "The preacher man is back in them woods, with Mort, my pard. Mort's dead, the preacher man is hurt bad but alive."

Both Dehner and the sheriff noticed the emphasis Browder had placed on *the preacher man is hurt bad but alive.* He wanted to prod them to immediate, thoughtless action.

"Where's the rest of your gang?" Bently snapped.

"Dead. Butch got killed in town two nights

183

ago. Mort killed Tobe to get a bigger cut of the money. Mort and me kidnapped the preacher man but he pulled a surprise; shot me with a Derringer and ran into the woods. Mort went after him, brought down the preacher with a shot to his leg. Poor, stupid Mort, he didn't figger the preacher man had another bullet in his Derringer. Now, Mort is dead and the preacher man is bleeding somewhere in those trees."

Neither Bently or Dehner believed the outlaw's story but both felt a compulsion to take action. "Why don't you stay here, I'll check out the woods."

Ox nodded agreement with the detective's words.

Rance moved quickly but cautiously into the woods. Clyde followed behind him. At first the dog's tail wagged playfully. But the animal soon became more somber as they moved deeper into the wooded area. He seemed to sense the seriousness of the situation.

Rance stopped for a moment and assessed his surroundings. The area was overgrown with trees, some thick, some thin, all struggling for survival. Dehner could sympathize with their plight.

The ground was covered with leaves, most of them crisp. A mixed blessing: he could hear anyone moving in the woods but, of course, he could also be heard.

Dehner drew his Colt and listened carefully.

There was no movement. If a wounded Paul Colten was somewhere among these trees, he would be making noise of some kind unless he had passed out or unless . . .

The detective began to move through the woods his eyes scanning the surroundings for signs of danger. Clyde followed close behind.

Birds took off from one tree causing Dehner to look in that direction. Clyde looked in a different direction and began to bark frantically. Dehner hit the ground feeling the air from a shot as it streaked past the back of his head.

The detective lay still. He hadn't seen where the shot had come from. But the close trees amplified sound. Dehner heard a rifle levering and ignited a red-orange flame in that direction.

An anguished cry of pain sounded across the wooded area. "I got lucky or somebody's one fine actor. I wonder which," Dehner whispered to Clyde as he gave the dog an appreciative pat on the head.

The question received a quick answer. Sounds of erratic but fast footsteps cut through the woods. Dehner could spot glimpses of his adversary but the man was moving behind trees to the degree possible.

Dehner trailed behind cautiously. His enemy was wounded but still armed. Clyde stayed close to the detective.

The enemy broke out of the woods and began

to move up the hill. Dehner could hear the voice of Paul Colten shout, "Stop right there, Tobe, drop the rifle."

The detective moved past the trees and came upon a bizarre sight. The man Colten had called Tobe was standing on the hill with his rifle pointed at the pastor. Colten was standing in front of a dead man about three yards downhill from Tobe. Colten was bent over with his right arm cradled in his left. In his right hand was a gun.

"It's all over, Tobe!" Colten shouted. "Give yourself up!"

"And die by a rope!" the outlaw shouted in an accusing manner as if it were the pastor's fault he would hang.

"I'm giving you one more chance, drop the rifle."

Tobe leaned forward, his voice that of a child in a tirade, "Damn you to hell, Preacher, damn you to hell."

Tobe began to cry hysterically as he lifted the Winchester. Colten silenced him with one shot. The outlaw crumbled to the ground.

Dehner approached the outlaw cautiously but only out of routine. The detective needed only a cursory glance and a fast grip on the killer's wrist to confirm that he was dead.

"Paul, are you all right?" Dehner asked as he approached the pastor.

"I'm fine," Colten's eyes remained on the pistol in his hand, his mind seeing something very significant there. The pastor slowly let the weapon slip out of his grasp and hit the ground.

An anguished expression waved over Paul's face, "I pray to God I never have to kill another man."

Colten began to retreat inside himself again, but suddenly broke into a whimsical smile and looked down. Clyde was on two legs, leaning on the pastor and licking his right hand.

Chapter Twenty-Six

Lolly Farnum stepped into Doctor Fred Cranston's house carrying a tray. Rance Dehner was coming out of the doctor's surgery.

"Right on time," the detective declared, as he noted the restaurant owner was wearing her usual food stained apron, "Riley Browder just woke up. He can use some food."

Lolly set the tray on a small table in the waiting room. The table stood several yards away from the surgery. She lifted the towel that rested on top and handed Rance a cup of coffee from a tray crowded with food. "I thought maybe you could use this."

Rance almost grabbed the cup, "Thanks, I sure could."

"Sheriff Bently has already had his free coffee for the day," the woman spoke with mock grouchiness. "He came by the restaurant earlier, guess he's still doin' his mornin' round."

The detective nodded his head and spoke softly. "With Doc Cranston off delivering a baby, I'm in charge for the moment. I'll probably be here alone for a while. Poor Ox is probably being stopped and asked questions by curious citizens. The Wilseys posted the story of what happened yesterday and early this morning in front of the newspaper office."

"Ox tole me 'bout that, sounds pretty crazy." Lolly looked through the open door to the surgery. The patient was lying still in bed, unaware or indifferent to the conversation going on in the waiting room. She lowered her voice before continuing, "This Browder fella is gonna tell who's been payin' him to do all the killin's, seems like it was some kind of . . . devil worshiper?"

"Sure sounds crazy," Dehner agreed. "But Doc wants to keep Browder here until later today. The bullet only grazed him but he has lost a lot of blood. We'll be taking him over to the jail tonight. After he eats the supper you'll bring him, he has promised to name the Satanist responsible for all the deaths. He'll do this good deed as long as Scoop and Mandy Wilsey are on hand. They have promised him the story will appear on the front page of the newspaper."

Lolly shook her head in a confused manner. "That buzzard's gonna hang. Why should he care 'bout gettin' his name in the newspaper?"

Dehner took a sip of coffee and nodded his appreciation to the restaurant owner. "When an outlaw is caught and facing the noose, he changes. Some find religion, others, well . . ."

Dehner walked around a bit and looked carefully into the surgery where there was still little movement from the one patient inside. "Some rats want to make a big show of their hanging. They crave all the attention they can get. They

190

brag about their crimes, boast about not fearing death. They want everyone to be caught up in their final end."

"Sounds like this Browder fella is choosin' braggin' over religion." Lolly picked up a small bowl of oatmeal from the tray, stuck a spoon in it and handed the bowl to Rance. "That should tide you over for a while. Later on, stop at the restaurant and I'll give you steak and eggs on the house."

"Thanks, Lolly, give me a shout if you need any help." Dehner found the room's most comfortable chair and settled down with his oatmeal and coffee.

"Don't reckon that'll be necessary." Lolly picked up the tray and carried it into the surgery. As she approached the one occupied bed she noticed Riley Browder was still wearing almost all of his clothes. A bloodied shirt lay in a waste basket, near the screen Doc Cranston used when operating. Browder's jacket enveloped a chair near the foot of the bed. His boots stood beside the chair.

Lolly placed the tray on the bedside table and looked down at the patient. "I see you're awake."

Riley Browder looked at her through glassy eyes. "Yeh, still sorta groggy."

The restaurant owner gestured toward the tray. "Got some ham, eggs and potatoes, that'll fix you up. But first, I'm gonna do you a big favor."

"What?"

"I'm gonna pray with you, whether you want me to or not. Now, sit up in bed."

Browder cautiously followed the instructions. He lightly caressed the bandages on his stomach as Lolly placed an arm on his shoulder, bent down and whispered in his ear. "I have a gun for you."

She reached into a large pocket of her apron and handed a six-gun to the outlaw. "You're leavin' town right now."

"I'm weak," he whispered.

"You'll be a lot weaker when they dangle you from a rope."

"Don't even have shirt . . ."

"Button up your jacket, no one will notice." She reached into her apron pocket again and brought out a roll of bills. "This here is enough money to buy a store full of shirts."

"How much?"

"A hunnert dollars."

"You promised—"

"And you promised to torture and kill Paul Colten. You failed. Hell, when the story gets 'round 'bout yesterday, he'll be a damn hero."

"OK, OK, still don't know how I can get outta here, even with gun . . ."

"I got it figgered, hold on."

Lolly stood up straight and beamed a large, benign smile. "Of course, the Lord forgives all sins. Jus' speak into my ear that you're wantin' forgiveness and God will hear ever' word."

She bent down again and returned to whispering. "We'll put the jacket on you, then you walk outta here holdin' the gun on me, like I'm your prisoner. Kill Dehner, then let me go and run 'round back. There's a fresh horse waitin' for you there."

"Won't the law suspect you, I mean, the gun and the horse?"

"I can handle it. I got that fool sheriff tied 'round my finger. He'll never suspect me. I'll stall him long as I can to give you time to put distance between you and this town."

Riley Browder closed his eyes for a few seconds. The plan wasn't too crazy, he might make it up north yet. "OK, let's do it."

Browder opened his eyes as Lolly again rose up and smiled. "You've done some terrible things, Riley Browder, but those sins are forgiven and right now the angels are rejoicin' over a repentant sinner." She paused a moment then continued, "Why, you're shakin' with cold. Here, let me help you with your jacket."

As she stepped toward the chair a familiar voice stopped her. "Drop the gun, Browder. Lolly, turn around and forget 'bout any more surprises you might have in that apron of yours."

Ox Bently stepped out from one side of the screen holding a gun. Doc Cranston stepped out from the other side. The doctor was wearing a look of shock and anger.

Riley Browder smiled sadly at the weapon Lolly had given him. "Guess I'm not gettin' back to Montana after all," he mumbled and then dropped the gun to the floor as if saying good-bye to his last friend.

"You lied and helped set me up!" Lolly shouted. "All that talk 'bout the newspaper and all was lies!"

Browder gave Farnum a look of cold indifference that came from defeat. "What?"

Lolly yelled at her former henchman. "That story, it was posted in front of the newspaper office!"

"These are terrible times we're living in, Lolly Farnum, why you just can't trust the press, anymore."

The restaurant owner looked toward the mock-friendly voice that came from the doorway. "Dehner . . ."

"The oatmeal you gave me was cold. I left it and have been standing beside this doorway for a while. Too bad you didn't go into the theater, Lolly, you have a great stage whisper. People in the balconies could have heard you. Don't blame your hired help, this whole scheme was my idea."

Like Ox Bently, Dehner held a gun in his hand. Unlike the sheriff, Dehner's attention was completely on the arrest he was about to make.

Ox's face looked like he was staring into a private hell. Doc Cranston looked with concern at his friend.

Lolly also looked at Ox Bently but without sympathy. "Fools! All of you are fools!"

Dehner kept his amicable pose. "You're right, Lolly, we haven't been very smart. We just took for granted that the killer behind all of this was someone related to one of the outlaws Paul Colten brought to justice. Someone Paul had hurt. We were wrong. Innocent people were being slaughtered because of someone Paul had helped."

"Some help!" Torment twisted across the woman's face. "You shoulda seen Caleb's body. My son had been tortured to death. When them rustlers realized Caleb was a Texas Ranger, they decided to make an example of him!"

A tremor shot through the woman's body. She regained her composure and gazed toward Ox and the doctor. "Then came the funeral. All them fine church folks tellin' me Caleb was in heaven. I didn't want him in heaven I wanted him here with me!"

Her eyes seemed to be looking at images inside her head. "And he would have been here except for that damned book by Paul Colten. My son got religion and got killed on account of it. Damn Paul Colten!"

Dehner's voice lost the false cheerfulness and

became neutral. "Was that when you became a Satanist?"

"I wanted to destroy Paul Colten and didn't care how I did it!" Lolly began to breathe deeply as if finishing a race. "I told the devil that if I could destroy Colten he could have my soul. And, unlike the goody-goody stuff you hear in church it worked!"

"What do you mean?" Dehner asked.

"A few months after I prayed to Satan, Paul Colten arrived in this town. Oh, by then, he was Reverend Colt the famous gunslinger. He left town after gettin' rid of some trash. But he came back to help build a church. By the time the church was built, I'd saved enough money to hire my own killers."

Dehner quickly glanced at Ox Bently, then looked away. Ox looked like a man drained of hope, conviction or anything else worth having.

The detective continued, "You didn't just want Paul Colten killed you wanted him tortured."

"Yes!" Lolly Farnum screamed. She seemed to be almost relishing the chance to shred her false self and turn her hatred loose. "I wanted him to suffer like Caleb did and I knew how to do it. I'd make him see the people around him tortured and killed. And, oh, how I enjoyed it when I wore that hooded robe and carried a lighted torch into the church and later when I put that noose in the good preacher's office. He knew he was battlin' the powers of Hell."

Rance shook his head in disbelief. "All of those innocent people you paid to have killed."

The woman held her head up as if expressing pride. "Not one tear did I shed for those fools, those stupid goody-goodies. Jared Ward, I had his wife killed, then when he was sittin' alone in my restaurant I got him fired up 'bout the chinks. I created a near riot in this town that rattled Paul Colten somethin' awful."

"Where did Zeke Talbot fit in?" Dehner asked.

Lolly gave a contemptuous laugh. "He didn't really. He was lovesick over Jenny Wong. I convinced him Satan would bring her to him if he helped me out. He brought some red dye I needed for red hoods. The toy snakes was his idea. At first, I didn't think I'd use them but they worked out good. I made lots of red hoods. At the last moment Kid Madero refused to wear them. But they got used."

"So did Zeke Talbot," Dehner said.

"Yeh," Lolly admitted. "The kid started givin' me trouble." She looked at Riley Browder who was sitting on the bed, staring at his clenched hands. "I had this buzzard kill Talbot and dump his body in the church."

"I think we've heard enough for now." Dehner looked at the sheriff. "If it's OK with you, Ox, I'll take Lolly over to the jail. You and

Doc can decide how to handle Riley Browder."

Ox remained silent, not even acknowledging Dehner had said anything. After an awkward silence, Doc Cranston spoke up. "Sure, we can handle this no good, go ahead Rance." He walked over and picked up the gun Browder had dropped to the floor. "We'll be bringing Riley Browder over to where he belongs in a few hours."

Ox watched intently as the detective took Lolly Farnum by the arm and led her out of the room. She never looked back.

Chapter Twenty-Seven

Rance could sense the tension as he and Ox stepped into the Wilsey home. Along with Mandy and Scoop Wilsey, Paul Colten was also there to greet them. This was supposed to be a happy, social occasion but Lolly's arrest the day before had pushed Ox deep into a personal isolation. He spoke only when necessary and always in a quiet monotone.

Mandy smiled at the sheriff as she pointed to Dehner. "Ox, can't you talk this man into staying in town just a little longer? I want to interview him for the *Grayson Herald*."

A wan smile was all the response Mandy received.

Paul Colten spoke into the silence. "There are some great smells coming from the kitchen!"

"I baked some cookies for Rance's little good-bye party," Mandy explained. "I'll fetch them along with some coffee. The rest of you, please sit down and make yourselves comfortable."

The four men did exactly as instructed. Scoop sat on a sofa where obviously his wife would be joining him. The other three men perched on nearby armchairs facing the sofa and surrounding the table in front of it. Rance mused that except for the presence of Paul Colten this was the same group that had assembled after the shootout with Kid Madero and his henchmen. Of course, back then Ox Bently was, well, Ox Bently.

Scoop tried to maintain the aura of cheerfulness. "Rance, can't you stay with us for another day or so?"

"No. I've got an important job and I need to get started today."

"What's that?" Paul Colten asked.

"Ox and I found the money from the stagecoach hold-up at the outlaw's camp yesterday. We also found the money they stole after murdering Rebecca. That money will be turned over to Rebecca's son. As for Wells Fargo money, I telegraphed my boss at the Lowrie Agency as soon as we returned to town. He got back to me this morning. I need to take the money to Shelbyville, about a day and a half ride from here. Wells Fargo has a major station there and they will have agents waiting to accept the loot."

Colten looked surprised. "One man carrying all that money . . . sounds dangerous."

"Not really," Dehner assured the pastor as he patted the saddlebags he had carried in with him which now lay at his feet. "Not many outlaws will be expecting a lone rider to be carrying a thousand dollars on him." He looked at Scoop. "Do me a favour and wait a week or so before mentioning all this in the newspaper."

There was good natured laughter from everyone except Ox. Mandy returned with a large tray containing cookies and coffee. As she placed the tray on the table, Dehner almost joked he was glad she wasn't wearing an apron. But a quick glance at Ox stopped him.

After making sure everyone had all the refreshments they wanted, Mandy sat down beside her husband and opened with a question. She wouldn't ignore the issues everyone was thinking about. She figured to do so would do more harm than good. "Rance, did you find anything unusual when you searched through Lolly's rooms?"

"Not much, as you know Lolly's rooms were in the back of the restaurant. I found a pentagram under her bed, that's an object used in Satan worship. She probably hung it on the wall when she held one of her . . . whatever you call it."

Scoop addressed Dehner before taking a bite from his cookie. "How did you come to suspect Lolly Farnum in the first place?"

"I owe it all to a cat named Wild Bill!"

"I don't follow you," Scoop admitted.

"Yesterday I stopped at Sammy's Hotel and Restaurant. While I was talking with Sammy a black cat jumped up on his counter. The cat was such a frequent visitor that Sammy gave him a name."

"Wild Bill," Paul Colten said.

The detective continued. "Exactly. Sammy told me he fed Wild Bill and the cat would come by from time to time then vanish for a few days."

"That's common behaviour for a stray cat," Mandy said.

"Yes," Dehner agreed, "and I figured Wild Bill also spent time at Lolly's Fine Eats. Lolly had even told people she fed stray cats."

Mandy's eyebrows shot up. "Wait a minute, is Wild Bill the same black cat that terrified Rebecca Locke?"

"Yes," the detective answered. "I recognized him from your newspaper story. Then I wondered why a stray cat would wander from an area where he was being fed daily out to a ranch."

"He didn't wander!" Scoop declared, as he realized where Dehner's account was heading. "Lolly scooped him up and took him out to the Locke ranch. Poor Rebecca was superstitious to begin with and in a bad state mentally with Wild Bill's strange looking face . . ."

Mandy finished her husband's thought. "Rebecca thought Wild Bill was Satan."

Dehner nodded his head. "The way I see it, Lolly went out to the Locke place the day before she took you out there, Mandy. She placed the cat in the house where, being daytime, it probably curled up and went to sleep. At night it began to prowl around and Rebecca saw it."

"Sneaking the cat into the church last Wednesday night wouldn't have been too tough either,"

Paul Colten noted. "Lolly fed Wild Bill and he probably trusted her as much as a cat trusts anyone."

"Yes, and a lot of little things began to come together," Dehner said. "For example, Ox took the business for providing food for prisoners away from Sammy and gave it to Lolly. Ox sensed Lolly's financial situation was tight. But why was she short on cash? Her restaurant was doing well. Lolly was saving every dollar she could in order to employ hired killers."

Mandy still looked confused. "Rance, yesterday you were running to the church to see Reverend Colten when I stopped you. I was looking for Clyde—"

Dehner cut in. "After I figured out the story on Wild Bill, I remembered Lolly had supposedly set up a meeting for Paul at the Ward ranch. Of course, she was really setting him up to be captured and killed. I ran to the church to stop him when you told me he was gone and Clyde was missing."

"And you figured Clyde had been kidnapped in order to get Paul to go along with their plans," Mandy concluded.

"That was a big mistake," Colten almost shouted. "Clyde barked just in time to warn Rance he was about to be shot. Clyde is a hero!"

Ox managed a weak but genuine smile at the pastor's remark. Mandy spotted the smile and tried to keep it there. She looked down at Clyde who stood by the table sniffing the aroma of the fresh baked cookies and wagging his tail. "OK, our hero will get a reward." She gave a cookie to Clyde who joyfully began to consume it.

The woman inhaled and pressed her lips together, "Rance, I hate to bring this up but, I guess it's the journalist in me, I have to know . . . the murder of Rebecca Locke . . ."

"You were set up, Mandy," Dehner replied immediately. "After you left the house, Zeke Talbot, who had been hiding nearby, stabbed Rebecca. Lolly not only got Rebecca fired up about Satan, she got the poor woman to confide where she and her husband locked up their money. Lolly and Zeke found the cash, Zeke hit Lolly just hard enough to back up the story she would tell, then he set the house on fire. Zeke fired shots to get your attention and get you back to the house."

"How can you be sure it was Zeke who helped Lolly and not one of that gang she hired?" the newspaperwoman asked.

"I can't," Dehner confessed. "And I can't be sure Lolly wasn't the one who stabbed Rebecca. But Zeke does seem to be the likely candidate. Lolly would have trusted him more. At the time, Zeke still believed Satan would deliver Jenny Wong to him. He would have been easy to maneuver."

"That Satan stuff, Lolly never believed it, not really."

Ox's statement stunned his four companions. Those were the first words Ox had spoken without prodding since the arrest of Lolly Farnum.

Mandy spoke softly as if a loud voice might push the sheriff back into isolation. "I don't understand, Ox."

"When she lost Caleb, her boy, somethin' snapped inside Lolly. Yeh, she acted natural but she was outta her mind." Ox was talking to the people in the house but his eyes were set on his twitching hands. "On Monday a U.S. Marshal is comin' ta take Lolly to Houston. They got a women's prison there and they gotta lot more."

Dehner tilted his head in a quizzical manner. "Now, it's my turn not to understand, Ox."

"Ya can't be found guilty of a crime ya did when ya weren't in your right mind," the lawman explained. "There's a lawyer in Houston who takes cases like Lolly's. I'm gonna hire him to defend her."

The sheriff's companions exchanged quick glances. A wild variety of thoughts were communicated in those glances: the lawyer would cost a lot of money, Ox Bently could spend the rest of his life worrying over a woman who was a mass murderer, his existence could become sad and hopeless.

The sheriff didn't sense the unease of his

companions. He continued to speak, half to himself. "The lawyer may want some of ya ta testify in court. Now, I don't expect ya to say anythin' but the truth. But if ya could jus' agree ta testify if the lawyer asks ya."

The lawman could see his friends nodding their heads. He nodded back in appreciation. "Lolly can never be free, not after all the things she done. But she should be put in an institution for people like her. She shouldn't go to prison and she shouldn't hang."

Ox Bently bowed his head and covered it with his hands. Mandy walked over to the sheriff, placed an arm around his shoulder and whispered something to him Rance couldn't hear.

Ox inhaled deeply, then sat up straight. "I should be gettin' back to work. Sorry ta ruin the party."

"You didn't ruin a thing, Ox," Dehner said as he picked up his saddlebags and tossed them over his shoulder. "I should be moving on myself."

Everyone, including Clyde, began to amble toward the front door. As they got outside and went through the front gate, Ox looked at the ground then looked up and directly faced Dehner. "Ya done a fine job, Rance."

"Thanks."

"I know I talked kinda rough to ya since . . . yesterday . . . but ya did what was right."

Ox turned abruptly and began to walk toward

the sheriff's office. His companions remained by the fence, watching him with concern. "That man has done a lot for this town," Paul Colten said. "Now, it's time for all of us to repay the favor."

Rance Dehner continued to watch the sheriff. Ox's steps seemed meandering and uncertain as if he were seeing Grayson for the first time.

The detective recalled his first meeting with Ox Bently. The lawman stood behind a desk cluttered with official documents, a newspaper, sarsaparilla and candy. The gentle giant was a man who, with good natured humor, took on any challenge a violent land could throw at him. A man dedicated to helping others and making a town safe for everyone.

And Dehner hoped someday that man could find his way back.

| Books are produced in the United States using U.S.-based materials | Books are printed using a revolutionary new process called THINKtech™ that lowers energy usage by 70% and increases overall quality | Books are durable and flexible because of Smyth-sewing | Paper is sourced using environmentally responsible foresting methods and the paper is acid-free |

Center Point Large Print
600 Brooks Road / PO Box 1
Thorndike, ME 04986-0001 USA

(207) 568-3717

US & Canada:
1 800 929-9108
www.centerpointlargeprint.com

LP W Clay James
Clay, James
Satan's guns : a western adventure